I0662818

Are You
Watching Me?
A Clive Dufault Mystery

M JOSEPH MURPHY

Are You Watching Me?

Copyright © 2016 Council of Peacocks Press
All rights reserved.
Editors: Maer Wilson (2nd Edition), Jae Blakney (1st edition)
ISBN 978-1-987811-07-0

Cover design by M Joseph Murphy
M Joseph Murphy's Official Website: mjosephmurphy.info

First Edition: March 2016, Second Edition 2019

This is a work of fiction. All of the characters, organizations, and events portrayed in this novel are either products of the author's imagination or are used fictitiously.

PREFACE TO THE SECOND EDITION

"This is a work of fiction. Names, characters, businesses, places, events, locales, and incidents are either the products of the author's imagination or used in a fictitious manner. Any resemblance to actual persons, living or dead, or actual events is purely coincidental."

If you're like me, you've seen this statement so many times it barely registers any more. Of course, we know it's just a book or just a movie. Writers often base their books on real events and real people. They change story details and the character names just enough so they're not recognizable.

That's not what happened with my book.

I started writing *Are You Watching Me?* as a NANOWRIMO in 2014. It took me a few years to write, not because it's a long book, but because it's dark. It was difficult for me to get in Clive Dufault's mind space and, once I finished, even harder to get out of it. There were difficulties with finding the right editor and pre-existing deadlines for my other book series. So, the book wasn't published until 2016.

In January of 2018, the real world got a little too close to my fictional one.

Are You Watching Me? is a fictional account of a serial killer in Toronto targeting gay men. The murders are brutal and involve bondage. One of the victims worked in a bar. All fairly generic, innocuous points until Bruce McArthur was arrested.

In January 18, 2018, Bruce McArthur, 66, was arrested for the murder of multiple men. They burst into his apartment as he was, apparently, about to kill another. As I write this, he's pled guilty to eight murders, although there could be more. He had been killing people since the 1970s.

Reality sucks. If you've read the first edition, you already know *Are You Watching Me?* is a paranormal thriller with hints of an evil not of this world, an evil that plays a great part in the books of my Activation Series.

Like many, I'd heard rumors about a serial killer in Toronto targeting gay men. For years, it was like an urban legend, right up there with alligators in the sewer or Chupacabra. People in the community spoke about it in whispers, but most didn't actually believe it.

When a real murderer was arrested, I felt sick. I took *Are You Watching Me?* off my social media feeds. I love this book, but I absolutely knew I couldn't promote it when the McArthur story was all over the news. I stopped all marketing on all my books. Of everything I've published,

I'm most proud of *Are You Watching Me?* And I felt pressured to let it slink into obscurity.

In the preface to his short story collection, Night Shift, Stephen King answers the question why he chooses to write horror. His answer:

"Why do you assume that I have a choice? Writing is a catch-as-catch-can sort of occupation. All of us seem to come equipped with filters on the floors of our minds, and all the filters have differing sizes and meshes. What catches in my filter may run right through yours."

Serial killers get stuck in my filter. They scare the shit out of me, more than any fictional monster, because they're real. Anyone could be a killer, even the gentle old man who dresses up like Santa Claus. And the more I looked into McArthur, the more freaked out I got.

The serial killer in my novel finds people through social media. So, did McArthur.

My hero, Clive Dufault, lives in Thorncliffe Park because one of my best friends, Gabe, lived in an apartment there for years. I visited him and stayed at his apartment often. Talking to his Torontonian friends was the first time I heard rumors of a gay serial killer.

Bruce McArthur lived in the same building as my friend. At the same time.

Being in that Thorncliffe Park complex, all those years ago, gave me an idea for a story that is a little too close to reality for my liking.

Once I learned that, I completely shut down. My mind went to very dark places. Could I have seen McArthur in the hallway? On the elevator? Was I visiting Gabe on a night McArthur murdered one of his victims? Is that why the story sank into my subconsciousness, urging me to write it?

Of course, this is crazy talk. The odds are very small I would have run into McArthur. That apartment complex is huge. And it's not like they were neighbours. Gabe lived in the same building but on a different floor.

For months, I stopped writing entirely. I knew I had to do something but what?

I decided to revise my book. I couldn't ignore the real murders. I needed, somehow, to do justice to the victims. So, I focused on the righteous anger of the gay community. For decades, the community in Toronto had asked police to investigate numerous suspicious disappearances. The police did not take them seriously. They fucked up because gay lives are expendable, especially those with brown skin. It's the main reason why police in Toronto have been un-invited from the Gay Pride parade.

I'm just a writer. I can't change the way society assigns value to people. I can't erase racism or homophobia, but at the very least I can shine a light on them.

I thought of revising my book to make it less similar to the real events, but that serves no one. I have an opportunity to tell a story that no one else is telling. Gay men died because society didn't care they went missing. If we'd cared a little bit more, maybe we would have caught McArthur before he killed so many.

This is a work of fiction. The similarities between my book and reality are purely coincidental. At the very least, they are unintentional. On the other hand, my commentary on the relationship between the police and the gay community for this second edition is completely intentional.

CHAPTER ONE

There's something addictive about fear. Seductive. The tingling in your stomach. The way your throat clenches. Your whole body tenses, poised for fight or flight. Your eyes blink faster. Your hearing becomes more acute. And you wait. Wait for the thing to happen.

A part of you wants it to happen.

Tonight, there's only one other passenger on the subway car: a balding Chinese man in a crumpled suit. He sways in his seat and his face is all red. My guess? He's wasted. I doubt he even sees me. I could do anything right now and he wouldn't even notice.

As quietly as possible, I unzip my winter jacket and reach into my inner pocket for my phone. Keeping my eyes on the Chinese guy, I activate the camera icon and switch to video. The guy slumps further into his seat and I press record.

As always, I start by sweeping the camera around the car to document where I am. Location is important. I lean the phone against my gym bag on the seat beside me. I take a few seconds to make sure the lens is focused on my crotch. This is when it gets exciting.

Eyes straight ahead, I slide my hands under the gray fabric of my jogging pants. I cup my balls for a moment, so warm against my cold hands. I slide my pants down and my cock pops up, exposed for the camera. I don't look down at the phone and keep my face blank. If I'm going to get away with this, I can't draw attention to myself. Not that it matters. In the city, no one really sees you.

I start with slow strokes and keep my breaths shallow. It takes me two seconds to get a semi. I stroke faster and grunt.

Drunk Chinese guy's eyes flicker open. He turns to stare at me, frowning.

What do you know? I was wrong. He did notice me. Cool.

There's a seat back between us. I'm pretty sure he can only see me from the chest up. I stop stroking and look forward with that bored zombie expression everyone in the city has. A second later, he loses interest in me and closes his eyes again.

Tons of people do that, dose off between subway stops, especially this late at night. I've never been able to. What can I say? I have trust issues.

I'm fully hard now. I bite down on the inside of my cheek so I don't make more noise. We're nearing my exit and I don't have much time. But I don't need long. Not like this. All Chinese guy has to do is stand up and he'll see what I'm doing. See everything. Maybe he would scream in disgust, call the police. Maybe run away. Maybe punch me. Kick me.

Part of me hopes he does.

Of course, there's this annoying little voice in the back of my head telling me to stop. It whispers that I'm not a teenager anymore. What I'm doing is sick. Perverse. Adults are supposed to know better. But that's just centuries of conditioning. I read on a forum once that humans are the only animals that don't have sex in public. Maybe that's why we're all so messed up. It's like we live in foggy bubbles, barely seen by anyone around us.

I'm not sick. I'm proving a point.

I'm close. For a second, I shut my eyes. Biological instinct: the urge to give myself over to the pressure building in me. But I force my eyes open and push my pants down further. This has to be seen. As I explode, I turn slightly towards the camera. I need it to capture the moment as it spurts out across the seat back in front of me. I dip my fingers in it, scooping up a sample to hold before the camera as evidence.

With my clean hand, I pan my phone around the car again. Drunk Chinese guy is still in dreamland.

I stop recording and put the phone back in my inner pocket. I pull out the special blue rag from my backpack, wipe off my dirty hand and pull my pants back up. I almost cleaned the splatter off the seat back but decided against it. Better to leave it. A surprise for someone else.

I snicker.

Drunk guy looks over at me again.

Oops. Didn't mean to laugh aloud. But I'm excited. I finally did it. I've been working up to this for months. I started with secluded places – alleyways and parking lots in the middle of the night. After that it was changing rooms at the mall, but not all malls. The new ones have security cameras. But then I saw these videos online – people all over the world jerking off on subways. At first it seemed so random and stupid. Now, it's all I can think about.

Five times. That's how often I rode this train late at night before I actually followed through. Each previous time I chickened out. But now I've done it – conquered my fear. Something tells me there's no going back.

The creepy subway voice says we're approaching Finch Station. I grab my backpack and go stand by the exit. Not that I'm eager to be back on the street. This is just more conditioning. Habits built up over time. The bell dings and you wait in line. Truth is, it's miserable up there, and I need to walk for a bit to catch the bus that will take me the rest of the way home. This is day three of what the networks are calling Snowmageddon. It's not that bad, really, but I'm sure the name helps sell papers. Schools close. There's a rush on salt. And for a brief moment everyone pretends they care about the homeless.

The train stops, the doors open, and I head towards the stairs. The station is empty this time of night, so I don't have to navigate a crowd.

They say crazy people don't realize they're crazy. If I know I'm a little nuts, I must be okay, right? I know normal people don't do what I do. I'm pretty sure Dr. Phil would say public masturbation isn't healthy. But honestly, who gives a fuck what Dr. Phil says? And so what if it's a tad illegal? Nothing makes me feel more alive than this. So completely present in the now. For a few blissful moments, nothing else in the world matters. Not my crappy job, my fucked-up past. Not even global warming.

In case you're wondering, my name is Clive Dufault. I'm twenty years old. A Sagittarius. I have blond hair and brown eyes, and yeah, I like to jerk off in public. But that's only the first part. As soon as I get home, I'll upload my video to a tube site, OutTube.com. If you don't know what a tube site is, think of it like YouTube filled with nothing but free porn. Every day, thousands of people like me all over the world film themselves having sex. Thanks to the

Internet, we have a place to share our adventures. Some people even make a living at it. Don't ask me how. I've got like thirty-seven followers and make zero money, but I do average a few thousand hits per upload.

It's nice to have fans.

Of course, I don't use my real name on the site and my face is always hidden. I haven't worked up the nerve to come out yet.

At the base of the stairs heading up, I take out my phone and launch the music app. I'm about to put in my blue tooth earbuds when I hear something behind me.

Heavy boots scraping across a dusty floor.

I look behind me. There's no one there.

It's probably just the Chinese guy. This is the last stop, so he must have gotten off.

Still . . .

"Fuck it." I shove my phone and earbuds away and hurry up the stairs. It's probably nothing, but I ignored my instincts once. It didn't end well. It feels like there's someone back there, watching me, hunting me, so I'm going to act like there is. Get to my safe place. My rational brain tells me I'm paranoid, but when you've lived through what I have, there are some chances you don't take. This is Toronto, after all. This city is full of psychos.

As soon as I'm back on the street, the feeling is gone. It's nearly 11:00 p.m. on a Wednesday night. Despite the snow, there are still pockets of people everywhere. They say New York is the city that never sleeps, but Toronto could give it a run for the money. Or title. You know what? Screw it. I think I screwed up that metaphor. Is that even a metaphor? I've never been what you'd call good with words. Maybe that's why things didn't work out for me at college.

The wind bites right through my coat, making me wish I lived on a tropical island, but I like the way the snow looks. The way it hides the dirty parts of the city. Everything looks cleaner, untouched. Besides, Christmas decorations look stupid without a little snow on the ground.

At the corner, I'm standing in a puddle of strangers. Something makes me look over my shoulder again. I catch movement near the subway exit, like someone ducked down to avoid being seen.

Hmm . . .

The light changes, and everyone crosses the street except me. I keep watching, waiting for some sign that there's someone there, hiding. I realize how monumentally stupid that is and race to lose myself in the crowd. Most likely I'm overreacting, but better safe than sorry.

Once I'm in the crowd again, no one notices me. It's like I'm invisible. My apartment is in an area called Thornhill.

It's not really close to the subway, so I have to take a bus the rest of the way. Counting bus trip and walking time, it takes me another twenty minutes to get home. By the time I get to my apartment door, I've almost forgotten about the person who may or may not be following me.

CHAPTER TWO

When I wake up the next morning, the first thing I do is regret every decision I've ever made. Why can't I get to bed on time? I drag myself to my computer and check the stats on the video I uploaded to OutTube.com last night. It's featured on the front page of the solo public sex section under recent releases. Bonus. Only two hits so far, but it's early.

After showering, I put on a pair of khakis and a gulf shirt for work. The shirt hangs loose on me because I'm built like a freakin' broom handle. I'm like anorexic skinny. I shouldn't say that, but I'm allowed to make inappropriate jokes in my own head.

On the elevator I run into the hot chick who lives on the floor above me. Her name's Amy, and unfortunately, she's a lesbian. Damn. That's also an inappropriate thing to say. But she's so flippin' hot. Short blond hair in what I think is called a pixie cut and apple-sized breasts with these huge ass nipples. She has a slim face and large blue eyes, like a walking talking hentai girl

"Morning, Clive," she says. "Did you see the news?"

"Nuhhuh." I punch the close button and the elevator door shuts. "Late night. Any word on the investigation?" It's an educated guess that's what she's talking about. Amy is obsessed with the recent murders of two gay men in the Toronto area. The first victim was the ex of one of her brother's friends. Or something like that.

"Worse," she says. "They found another body. Doesn't that freak you out?"

"Of course," I say. But it really doesn't. So what if there's a gay serial killer in town? I'm not gay, and none of my friends are gay. Except Amy, who I guess could be called a friend, but she's also a chick, so probably safe. I also realize normal people don't say things like that. That type of honesty isn't socially acceptable, so I say what Amy expects to hear. "Sounds more and more like a serial killer. Hard to believe we have one here, though, eh?"

Yes, I said "eh." I'm Canadian. It's allowed.

Amy shivers visibly. "People say the police aren't looking into it as much as they should because only gay people are dying."

"People suck." My mind turns to a moment frozen in time. Blink. I am twelve years old, screaming. I see the knife. Blink. I'm back in the present. I take out my phone and pull up Facebook. I need a distraction to shut that shit down. No time to deal with psychic scars. I have to get to work.

The door opens. We both step out of the elevator and head into the lobby.

"Who was it?" I ask, because I know I'm supposed to care. "Anyone you know?"

She shakes her head, slowly like she's disappointed. "No. I don't think so. The name and picture weren't familiar, but you know how small this city is. Everyone's connected. Just like with Michael. You remember, my friend? The first victim."

Suddenly he's a friend now? I know what she's doing. I've seen this before. She's trying to make herself appear more important by claiming a relationship with the dead guy. It's pathetic. I'd still fuck her, though.

I nod. "Of course I remember."

"You have to read the articles online. So creepy. They found this new body tied to a chair in front of a window, strangled with plastic rope. Who does that?"

I shake my head. "It's a crazy world out there."

Unfortunately, I know all too well that the world is full of people doing unimaginable things. And it's usually the people you least expect, the ones who look the most normal.

Amy waves bye and walks over to the security guard. She asks him something, and he nods towards the door. She crosses her arms like she's angry, but he just points at his watch. She flicks her wrist, dismissing him. She takes out her cell phone and walks away.

Looks like someone is pissy today.

After a quick bus ride, I'm back in the subway. It's swarming with people, hundreds of unknown faces in all shades and hues. It's one of the things I love about Toronto. So many people completely focused on their own existence. Not one of them will see what I'm about to do.

It's standing room only. I find a spot in the middle of the car. My left hand holds the bar above my head for stability. My right is on my crotch. I keep my eyes straight ahead, not looking at anyone, not focused on anything. I stroke my thumb up and down my balls, slowly at first but faster as my dick hardens. My peripheral vision is focused on a Korean woman with her long black hair in a ponytail. What I wouldn't give to—

Someone elbows me in the rib cage. Hard.

I turn around to snap at them, but I can't figure out who it was. We're all so cramped together it could have been anyone standing near me. The young guy in the expensive suit. The tiny Somalian woman with the shaved head and piercings. The half-asleep teenager with the Beats headphones.

No one looks back at me, no apology, no confrontation. No use getting upset. This sort of thing happens all the time on public transit.

It takes twenty minutes to get to work. Same as always. I work in customer service at a call center for one of the big banks. On paper, I deal with customer complaints and questions about their accounts. Mostly, I try to upsell them new credits cards or investments. The work doesn't completely suck and the money's okay, so I don't complain.

I work on the twentieth floor, and I'll never be bored enough to walk up. As I push the up button to call the elevator, I hear someone call my name.

"Hey, Clive."

I smile, recognizing the voice. "Hey, Delilah."

She comes from behind to stand beside me, and I force the smile away. Delilah has this whole Amy Lee vibe: heart-shaped face and pale skin. She's a little over five feet tall with long hair died blue-black and thin lips painted blood red. With her wide hips and oversized breasts, she's like a gothic fertility goddess in blue jeans. I feel the heat of her body whenever she's close to me. I can tell she's totally got a thing for me, but even I have limits. Never sleep with a girl you work with. Never.

"Did you hear the news?" she asks.

I nod. "Another murder. Weird, huh?"

"Yeah." She touches the chain around her throat, straightening the crucifix. "My mom is freaking out. She never wanted me to move into the city. I told her Toronto is safe, but . . ."

"Toronto is safe." I place my hand on her shoulder and watch her eyes light up. Whoops. Stop flirting, Clive. Remember, you're at work. "We have one of the lowest rates of violent crime in the world compared to other big cities. Besides, if there is a serial killer, both you and I are safe."

"How you figure?"

I hesitate for a moment, reminding myself to phrase this carefully. "I mean, look at the pattern. Three gay guys including the one this morning. So unless you're a guy in drag you have nothing to worry about." I look at her breasts for a moment, confirming that she is one hundred percent woman. "And neither do I."

Delilah blushes, and I wonder if she noticed me looking at her boobs. I swear, women have a sixth sense for that kind of thing.

"You're probably right," she says. "Clive, can I ask you a question?"

Uh oh. I recognize that tone of voice. She's about to ask me out.

"Oh." I slap my forehead. "I forgot to get coffee. Can you punch in for me? I'm going to run to Starbucks. Can I get you something?"

Delilah deflates, her eyes focused on the ground. "No. That's fine. I'll see you later."

I smile at her and walk away. The crowd swallows her up and I feel relieved. It's not that I don't like Delilah. Truth is, I like her a lot. If we didn't work together something would definitely happen. But it would be short. And painful. I've never been what you'd call good with women. All I seem to know how to do is disappoint them.

It's only when I'm ordering coffee that it hits me.

Amy never said the third victim was gay.

I assumed that because of past evidence. But what if I'm wrong? Maybe I'm not as safe as I thought.

***

Work is monotonous and stressful. Lots of people yell at me. Must be a full moon.

I take my 3:00 p.m. break in the employee washroom: time to check up on the stats for my newest video. I have to check from my phone because work monitors our computer browsing history. I flip the lid on the toilet down and sit, locking the stall.

I've got over a thousand hits now and five comments. Damn. It's never happened this quickly before. Guess the subway was the right location. I smile as I read the first two.

"Awesome."

"So hot."

But it's the third one I remember.

"So nice to bump into you on the subway this morning."

CHAPTER THREE

You know that moment in movies where people get scared and throw their phones? I totally have that moment but don't actually throw it because it's a flippin' iPhone and I'm not made of money. Instead, I stare at the words on the phone screen for I don't know how long. I snap out of it when I hear the bathroom door swing open. I slip my phone back into my pocket and flush the toilet to give the illusion I used it.

As I head back to my cubicle, I repeatedly tell myself the comment means nothing. Sure, I felt someone elbow me on the subway this morning, but that's a coincidence. There's no way anyone could recognize me from the videos I've put online. I never show my face. I doubt anyone could identify me from my clothes, either. Of course, there's my scars. I look at my hands: tiny white circles on the front and back of my palms are a constant reminder of the worst day of my life. Is that how they found me?

"Stop it, Clive," I mumble. "You're obsessing."

I forgot to mention. I have slight to moderate Obsessive-Compulsive Disorder, at least that's what the doctors told me. Most people confuse OCD with being a neat freak. Anyone who knows me can tell you I'm no neat freak. Real OCD is an anxiety disorder. For me, things get stuck in my head, and I can't ignore them. I have to do something – little daily rituals – or the thoughts keep looping. I clean my ears five times a day, which means I go through cotton swabs like nothing. When I'm home, I check the lock on the front door every time I walk by it, even if I've been inside all day. After washing my hands, I always use three paper towels to dry them. I'm not sure why I chose these rituals, but they don't interfere with my life. Not much, at least.

By the time I clock out of work, I've convinced myself the comment was left by the serial killer. He – or she – is an advanced hacker who has tracked down my IP address. I'm the next victim. In fact, I'm basically dead already. I can practically hear my mother crying at the funeral.

Rationally, I know I'm being ridiculous. Dr. Angus, my old psychiatrist, called this rumination, a fancy word for my mind latching onto a train of thought like a leech. The message plays on a continuous loop, sucking the life out of me. My rituals and recording my videos help, but Dr. Angus said the best cure, aside from medication, is Cognitive Behaviour Therapy. When I feel the loop starting, I need to consciously change my mental processes. I focus on problem solving: identify the distortion and use logic to see things as they really are. Rumination can consume my life. It was bad when I was teenager, but it's mostly under control nowadays.

So, let's look at the facts. Aside from being gay, what else did the victims have in common? Hmm. No idea. I don't even know the names of the dead guys. And since I don't know what they all have in common, maybe I do have something in common with them after all.

Stop it.

I take a deep breath and get back to logic. All the victims are gay. Aside from my perfectly natural man-crush on Chris Pratt – because who isn't a little bit in love with Chris Pratt? – I'm completely hetero. Assuming there really is a serial killer – which has not even been proven yet– they kill to make a point, to follow some sort of narrative or work on some psychological issues. The evidence doesn't support my fear.

You may be wondering why I know so much about serial killers. Let's just say I had a crash course.

The more likely scenario is that the comment was left by a troll, some idiot posting things on the internet just to rile me up. But there's nothing rational about obsession and compulsion. Dr. Angus told me it was about control, like maybe there was something in my past that made me feel like I wasn't safe and my OCD habits give me back a sense of control.

Gee, I wonder what that was?

I get out into the streets and I'm surrounded by strangers. I have this moment of extreme weirdness. I look at the faces of all these people, recognize none of them. Any one of them could have left that comment. Any one of them could be the killer.

"Stop!" I clench my fists and close my eyes.

The thoughts are trying to come back again. If I don't get this under control, I'll be back in the hospital. They'll force me to take those meds again.

I follow the throng down into the subway. I stand with my back to the wall as far from the tracks as possible. The air tastes like oil and dirt. It's hard to breathe. When the train arrives, I can't get on. My body refuses to move. I know this feeling. I'm heading towards a full-on panic attack. Recognizing this helps me snap out of it. In that way, I'm lucky. My OCD isn't as severe as other people's. I don't need the antipsychotics Dr. Angus prescribed. I refuse to live my life medicated. You ask me, doctors are nothing but pill pushers. I take deep breaths and remind myself that one comment doesn't mean I have a stalker.

I get on the next train.

Once I'm safely back in my apartment, I take out my phone to check my stats again.

The comment is gone.

I frown and put my phone away. Did I imagine the whole thing? No. That's not possible. I know it was there before. I'm not crazy. Well, not that type of crazy. Hallucinations aren't common with OCD.

Surprisingly, I'm disappointed. I think a part of me was starting to think it might be kind of cool to have a stalker. Not the Fatal Attraction type thing, of course, but someone who is completely obsessed with me. They would eat, drink and sleep me.

I take out the phone and check the comments again. Maybe I just missed it. Nope. Still gone. Nevertheless, as soon as I get home, I triple check that my front door is locked behind me.

***

"What about that one?"

This comes from my best friend, Kevin Nielson. When he's not so drunk he can barely stand, he kind of looks like he should be an Abercrombie and Fitch model. Girls love him, especially cougars. I should probably be jealous of him, too, but he's impossible to hate. We've been friends forever.

It's Thursday night and we're standing against the wall of this stupid club we go to. It's called Cube, and it's usually pretty lame. But it's less lame than the other shit places we go. A dance remix of a Sia song is playing as Kevin and I begin the hunt.

I shake my head. "She's got crazy, stalker eyes. You should go for the one in pink."

Kevin rolls his eyes. "Only if I was on crack. She looks like a soccer mom."

The woman he says looks like a soccer mom is maybe twenty-five. She has long curly hair, and she's wearing a pink sweater. She's smiling and looks extremely bored but not the fake kind of bored you see in the Kardashian-wannabes. She sincerely looks like she's waiting for something interesting to happen.

"I thought you liked soccer moms," I say.

"Only the real ones. Give me a woman in her forties any day."

I take a swig of my beer. "Maybe you should start going to bingo."

Kevin gives me a slow smile. "That's actually not a bad idea. Shots?"

Of course I say yes. After that, the night is mostly a blur of lights and sweaty bodies. Three shots later, I'm on the dance floor. I've lost Kevin, but that's usual. Last I saw, he was chatting up the woman with the crazy, stalker eyes.

They're playing an oldie – something by Nellie – when I catch her eye: soccer mom in the pink sweater. She's staring at me from the bar. I recognize that look, the way she licks her glossed lips. She's sending me a clear message: she is prey.

I smile back and let my monster shine out through my eyes. Just a little, enough to show her I'm a hunter but not enough to scare her. I think of my hunger like that sometimes, a demon inside me that needs to feed. And suddenly I don't want to feed on her. I need to.

She blushes slightly and turns away. She touches her hair and turns to talk to a friend – an athletic girl with long brown hair. When the friend turns to scrutinize me, I hide my beast. Friends can spot a hunter and steer the prey away. It's really not much different than animals in the wilds of Africa. If I look dangerous, the friend will tell the prey to flee. So, instead, I make my eyes wide and somewhat bewildered. Basically, I'm pretending I'm someone who can't believe they've been dragged into a night club. I watch as the soccer mom's friend nods in approval. Several women are nodding their approval, pushing soccer mom towards me.

The game is on.

I smile at her, and we start dancing. She touches her hair again. I'm pretending to be too shy to look her in the eye. I always love this part. Because it's totally fake. We're both playing a game and we know it. Of course, I'm lying to her about who I am just like she's lying to me. The whole dating world is built on nothing but lies.

At the end of the first song I lean in and shout my name so she can hear it over the music. I say thanks and when she asks for what I say for rescuing me from being alone. I tell her a partial truth. I've been abandoned by my good-looking friend, and I feel weird because I don't know anyone else here.

I can tell this is the right thing to say because she takes a step closer to me. I smell her sweat and her perfume. She pushes her shoulders back exposing more of her neck. I think about kissing it, but I can't spring my trap just yet. Too soon and you scare the prey.

I wait until the second song ends. I ask her if she wants to sit for a second, to talk. Asking if a girl wants a drink is so lame. What they really want is for someone else to see them, to hear to them, to be completely present with them.

So, I take her to a dark corner and listen.

Well, I don't really listen. It's more like when you're sitting in a class and you vaguely pay attention to what the teacher says in case you get pulled for random questions.

She tells me her name again. Tonia. She's from Ottawa, just in town for the weekend with her friend Jan, the athletic girl she was with earlier. Tonia's recently broken up with her boyfriend, Brian, because she caught him cheating. She's only twenty, and she's only ever been with one man before.

All the time she's talking I shut up and keep my eyes on her. I listen, nod when appropriate, scowl in disgust at Brian's betrayal. I keep a respectful distance and wait for her to signal me to come in closer.

Then, I see it, the moment she suddenly surrenders to me. Her lips part and she lowers her tear-damp eyes. I touch her cheek and say I'm sorry, tell her Brian is an idiot.

We kiss.

After this it's too late for her to escape. I've sprung my trap just as she's sprung hers. There's no way for me to know if she's telling the truth about this Brian dude, and honestly, I don't care. We both know where this is going. We both need it. All the talk now is only a game.

She introduces me to her friend, Jan who is less than thrilled that Tonia wants to go home with me. I spend thirty minutes convincing Jan I'm not a rapist. Jan mentions the serial killer, which just makes Tonia laugh. A few minutes later, Tonia and I leave.

We're sitting in the back seat of a cab. Tonia holds my hand all the way to my place, and this is another lie. It's fake intimacy. We both know there's no future here. She lives four hours away and is clearly not over her ex. If he even is an ex. For all I know, they're still together and I'm just a diversion.

I've had worse Thursdays.

We stumble into the lobby and the security guard shushes us. Tonia laughs and I apologize.

We are barely in my front door, and I have her pants off. I kneel before her, kissing and sucking the lips of her vagina. What were you expecting me to call it, something cute? Like her southern lips or quivering mound of love pudding?

It doesn't take long until she's moaning. She slams her palms against the wall, thrusts herself into my face. My tongue enters her more deeply and I feel like I'm in heaven. This is my drug, the greatest high. Making another person come is the most powerful thing you can do.

Tonia moans my name, tells me to fuck her. We tear off the rest of our clothes and race to my room. Her hands are behind her head as I put on a condom and slide into her.

I've never understood why some men rush this part. What the hell is the point of quick sex? I want this feeling to last forever.

Tonia is on top of me now. She bites the lower corner of her lip and moves faster. I watch in awe as I match her movement. Occasionally, I thrust extra hard, throwing her slightly off balance. She throws her head back and puts one hand on my chest. The entire world stops.

I wish I could feel what she feels. Instead, I feel removed from the scene, like the sex is something I'm watching rather than something I'm doing.

Tonia is cooing now, a soft erotic sound. Her body trembles and vaginal fluids coat me. She's oblivious to the entire world and suddenly I can't control myself.

I grab her hips for leverage and pound into her. Her eyes grow wide and, for a moment, her whole being is open to me. She isn't a stranger. I know every speck of her. She looks down at me and gives me a goofy smile like she's truly seeing me for the first time.

Then, it's over. She collapses beside me, sweat drenched and twitching. Her fingers trace the curves of my scrawny muscles and I turn away.

I stare at the wall. Numbness persistently spreads through me. The sex was magical. And now it's over. I count the seconds until she leaves.

***

Annoyingly, Tonia doesn't leave. She curls up and falls asleep. She looks utterly at peace clutching my sheets. The smell of her perfume and our sex is everywhere.

I want to escape but this is my apartment. I can't leave. Instead, I lie awake for hours until I hear her snoring. Slipping out of bed, I head to the bathroom.

I check my phone as I sit on the toilet. There's a text from Kevin. He's taken a picture of the woman he banged. She's sleeping, her big tits exposed, completely unaware he's taken a photo.

"Dirty dog," I say. It's not like Kevin to send me pictures like this. He must really like her.

I turn on the shower, making it as hot as possible. I scrub soap over my skin to remove every trace of Tonia. I need to feel clean again, because as beautiful as our moment was, I know it was all a lie.

I turn off the taps just in time to hear the door to my apartment open and close. Wrapping a towel around my waist, I head to my bedroom.

Tonia is gone.

There's no note, of course. No one leaves notes in the real world.

I grunt and shake my head. It's weird and completely irrational. Moments ago I wanted her gone, but I wanted to be the one to tell her to leave. She left, taking that power away from me. We are more alike than I thought. So, for no good reason, I'm heartbroken. And I miss her.

In the corner of my room is a full-length mirror. I star at myself, trying to really see me. You know in books how people look at their reflections for a long time? In reality, it's actually pretty difficult to just stand there and really see yourself. At least it is for me. My body doesn't seem real. Like what I see belongs to someone else.

I walk closer to the mirror, focusing on my eyes. It takes two seconds before I'm completely weirded out. It almost feels like someone is on the other side of the mirror looking back at me. I turn away, let my towel fall to the floor, and collapse in bed.

I fall asleep, breathing in the scents of Tonia, smiling at the memory of her moans.

CHAPTER FOUR

Sunday afternoon I get the nerve up to do another video. Maybe it's the pictures Kevin keeps sending me of this new girl he's seeing. All the pictures are at night when she's sleeping, which is honestly kind of creepy. But also kinda hot.

There hasn't been any weirdness for days. No encounters on the subway, no freaky comments on my videos. Life is pretty much back to boring normal. Time to get back on the horse, so to speak.

I head downtown to the Hard Rock Cafe. I eat lunch and then head to the bathroom. This isn't as high-risk as jerking off on a subway car, but if I tag it as Hard Rock Toronto I'm sure I'll get a ton of hits. I sit in one of the stalls and get out my phone. I drop my pants and start recording. I make sure to show that the stall door is still open, not much, but a crack. Otherwise, where's the risk? I hear the bathroom door open. Three guys come in talking about baseball and I start jerking off. Such a fucking thrill. I clench my jaw trying hard not to make a sound. I fantasize about being in the woman's washroom, but I haven't tried that yet. For some reason that seems like a violation, like I'm assaulting the women. There's no assault here, no harm. Just the risk of being caught.

I open the stall door a bit further. The guys are at the urinal. If they glanced back, they will see me. I turn the camera to show them, to prove where I am. The tension builds and builds and I explode. I want to scream, to moan, but I hold it all in. I close the stall door as one of the guys finishes at the urinal. When they exit, I pull up my pants and leave.

When I get home, I log into the tube site to upload my video. For a moment I hesitate, thinking again of that strange comment. But I push past it. Jerking off in public is all about conquering fear, pushing past societal conventions, to do what other people only dream of doing.

After I upload it, I head down to the laundry room. Amy is there talking with some guy who looks vaguely familiar. With his dark hair and olive skin, I peg him as Italian. He has the type of muscles you only see on underwear models or Olympic gymnasts. So, I basically hate him immediately. They're talking about the murders – of course – as she folds her laundry. I wave politely and load my clothes into a washer as far away from them as possible. The last thing my thin grasp on sanity needs is a conversation about a potential serial killer in town. I've finally got my thoughts under control again.

***

Monday morning, I wake up before the alarm. It's a good day. I actually get to work twenty minutes early. That never happens. Delilah heads to my desk and she has this awkward look on her face. Immediately, I want to cheer her up.

"What's up, beautiful?"

She blinks at me and shakes her head. "What's wrong with you? Aren't you freaked out?"

"Why would I be freaked out?" I look around, worrying for a second that I've missed some important environmental cue. Like a notice of termination pinned to a bulletin board or someone crying at their workstation.

"You can be so clueless sometimes, Clive. Didn't you notice all the police downstairs?"

I frown. "There were police?" I search my memory. "Sorry. I usually zone out before my first coffee. You know that. What happened?"

She leans closer to me, her voice a low whisper. "They found a body. Reba says one of the cleaners found it on the third floor last night."

"You mean the third floor here?" And there goes my good mood. I can practically see it slipping away. "In this building? Isn't that a law firm or something?"

Delilah nods. "Handler and Associates. I think they mostly do corporate law. Everyone's saying it might be another victim of the serial killer. I'm so freaked out I don't know how I'm going to get through this day. You hear about these things happening in America all the time, but to have it happen so close is . . ." She shivers.

"Hey." I reach out and touch her hand. "You're safe. I'm sure there's nothing to worry about. Fuck the people and their paranoid talk. You know how people get. They blow things out of proportion. If they found a body, odds are the guy died of natural causes. You know lawyer types. Super high strung. And if he was killed, statistics say most people are killed by people they know, not by strangers."

I hear snickering from behind me. I look over, and Corey, the loser in the cubicle across the aisle, is staring right at me. He winks. Only then do I realize I'm still touching Delilah's hand. I jerk my hand back. Delilah blushes.

"You're probably right," she says. "It's still creepy, though."

At work, the death is all anyone talks about for the rest of the day. I hear at least three different versions of what happened. The only thing each story agrees on is the guy's name, Jerry Tran. Two versions say he was found naked at his computer. Another one says he hanged himself with a tie, which I think is actually next to impossible unless it was one of those auto-erotic asphyxiation things gone wrong. The more people talk about it, the less interested I become. It's disgusting the way people get off on other people's tragedies.

I had something happen to me when I was a kid. An incident. I don't like to talk about it. When I was a teenager, I told a few people about it, trying to move past it. My therapists said talking about it is the first step to healing. Afterwards, it was all anyone wanted to talk about. How do I feel about it? Do I still have nightmares? Christ. How can you move past something when everyone around you is fixated on it?

I see the gleam in my coworkers' eyes as they discuss Jerry Tran and count myself lucky that nobody at work knows about my incident.

***

I have this little ritual I do when I get home. It's one of my things. Everyone with OCD has something they do. Some people wash their hands. Others rearrange their desks. As I said, I obsess over making sure the door is locked. Rationally, I know it will be locked when I get home because, when I leave, I always check it three times. I never walk away unless I hear the click of the mechanism locking. After that, I try to twist the knob. Finally, I try to push the door open. Only when I'm sure it's locked can I leave. It doesn't hurt anyone, and it helps me feel less anxious. No biggie.

Today when I get home, I twist the key and wait until I hear the click. Only after I hear it unlock can I be certain I locked it in the morning. If I don't hear the click when I unlock the door, maybe I forgot to lock it. Maybe someone broke into my apartment. They could be waiting for me in there, hiding in a closet with a knife and an ether-soaked rag. As soon as I hear the click I relax.

I turn the key and there's a faint but audible sound. I relax.

Mostly.

As I'm pulling things out of the fridge to start supper, part of me wonders if I really heard the click. Maybe I only wanted to hear it. Worse. Maybe someone broke in and relocked the door to fool me into thinking I really had locked it in the morning. They could be waiting in the bathroom right now, hiding behind the shower curtain. I sigh. There's only one way I'm going to be able to get past this. If I don't check the apartment, these stupid thoughts will be running through my head all night.

I live in a small one bedroom, so it doesn't take me long to go through it. I check under the bed, which is silly because there's maybe an inch of space there. I open the shower curtain and even open all the cupboards in the kitchen. Before you know it, I'm checking under my bed again. That's not a good sign.

I refuse to take pharmaceuticals. My rituals are stupid, but they don't disrupt my life. I've started taking natural remedies for anxiety disorders – daily probiotics and valerian root – and they usually work. But probiotics can be stupid expensive. I ran out last week and won't have the money to get more until next payday.

I stop myself from checking under the kitchen cupboards again and pop four valerian root pills. It will take at least an hour before that does any good, so I need to keep myself occupied. I take a steak out of the freezer and throw it into the microwave to defrost. I turn on my computer and surf some porn.

A quick look at my apartment will convince you I'm not a neat freak. The only thing I organize is porn. I'm up to forty gigs of images organized into files dependent on hair color, racial background, and activity. Essentially, I'm a porn curator. Whenever insomnia hits, which is often, this is one of the few things that quiets my mind enough so I can sleep. When that doesn't work, I listen to binaural sound waves on an old iPod. Because my ears are super sensitive, I use these things called sleep headphones which are really flat speakers inside of a headband that cost 80 bucks. I won't risk falling asleep wearing earbuds.

I eat supper and watch some TV. I stumble upon the national news. There's a black woman from Toronto Pride talking about the murders. She says the police aren't trying as hard as they should to find the killer because all the victims are gay. So there you go. The third victim was gay after all. Nothing about Jerry Tran so obviously his death has nothing to with the serial killer.

I call my mom just to say hi. She tells me about her week. I talk about work. She asks if I've met any girls. Annoyingly, I think about Delilah but tell her there's no one.

I play some video games, chat on Facebook for a bit and a thought forms in my mind: did I lock the front door? I know I did. I clearly recall turning the deadbolt and putting the chain in place, but this is part of my OCD. I recognize patterns or think I recognize patterns. My brain tricks me into thinking something is off, which triggers alarm bells. Sometimes I can ignore it. Other times, that part of my brain wonders if this is the time my instincts are right. Maybe something really is wrong and if I don't act on it . . .

"Crap." I get up from my computer and look at the door. As soon as I verify it's locked, I'm okay again. That tells me the valerian root is working.

Before bed, it's time to masturbate. I average about twice a day which is, according to Google, pretty average. If a guy tells you they don't watch porn and jerk off, they're lying. They're probably lying because they think about you when they're stroking. Doing it at home doesn't give me a high like it does in public places, but it takes the edge off. I'm on the tube site and do a search for women masturbating in public places. My people. First is a black security guard who fingers herself in a warehouse. Another is a cougar with gray hair straddling naked on a swing set in a park during the middle of the day. I find a woman in her twenties masturbating in a public library. That would take guts. The clips are mildly entertaining but they're not making me hard. Actually, I'm getting bored. So, I filter the search to show the highest rated videos only.

I find one with a couple fucking against the counter in a bathroom. The fingernail image strikes me as odd but I can't figure out why. I click the start button.

The man, an Asian, is naked, eating out the woman, a redhead. She has her hands behind her, one on the mirror, the other on the counter. Her head is thrown back and she's loud. It's hot in a way but my brain is all fuzzy. I can clearly tell something is off, but I can't tell what. It hits me.

I recognize that bathroom.

"Shit. Those are the washrooms from work." I click the pause button, staring at the details. I've seen those tiles, those faucets so often. I can't believe I didn't catch it sooner. My mind starts to race.

Asian.

"That guy . . . could that be the dead guy, Jerry Tran?"

I run my fingers through my hair and step away from the computer. "Get it together, Clive. You're being ridiculous. That bathroom could be anywhere in the world. What are the odds your building is the only one in the world with those tiles?"

Logically, I know they weren't custom made. Those tiles are probably in hundreds of other buildings around the world. That makes sense, right? And even if it is my building, this is Toronto. There are at least a hundred Asian men that work in my building. That's even assuming the guy in the video works in the building. Maybe the woman does. Or maybe they are part of the janitorial staff. Maybe it was from five years ago.

I go to the medicine cabinet and get four more valerian root pills. Don't worry. I'm nowhere near overdosing. I'm following the directions on the bottle. Sort of. But mostly I know when my anxiety is taking over. If I don't do this, I won't sleep at all tonight.

I grab a beer from the fridge and go back to the video. What if the guy in the video really is Jerry Tran? Maybe that's how the serial killer finds his victims. He already commented on mine.

"Stop it!" I smack my head and take a swig of beer. "Jerry wasn't murdered. And that wasn't the serial killer who made that comment. You're being ridiculous."

Still, I check the comment section. There are fifteen comments. Most of them are normal.

One sticks out.

"I warned you."

"Fuck." I close my browser and push my chair away from the computer.

Somehow, I don't think I'll be sleeping tonight.

CHAPTER FIVE

The morning is bad. I only got a few hours' sleep last night. My mind races to create ridiculous connections between unrelated events. I know I'm being irrational, and I don't act out. I mean, it's not like I'm cutting myself or running to the police with my crazy theories. Some people have OCD so bad they can't live a normal life.

I cope.

Calling in sick isn't going to happen because I refuse to let this thing rule my life. So, after I shower, I get dressed and eat breakfast like a normal person. But not before I check that the front door is still locked. I have time to watch the news this morning. More recaps on the latest murder victim. Still nothing on Jerry Tran. I pull out my phone and "Google Jerry Tran lawyer Toronto." Only thing I can find is his LinkedIn page with a picture of a smiling and very-well-dressed Asian man. I also find his blurb on the Handler and Associates' personnel page. He was a senior partner in his late forties who did a bunch of charity work. There's nothing anywhere online about his death.

That's actually a good sign. It makes it more likely that the death wasn't homicide. One of my cousins is a police officer in Ottawa and has the worst job ever. She responds whenever people find a dead body. Most of the time it's natural causes. They rarely make the paper except the obituaries. She told me that people who take their own lives almost never make the paper, either. Too many authority figures worried about copycats and suicide pacts. Murders, however, end up everywhere in the news because they're so rare.

"See. He wasn't murdered. Relax." Now that I'm convinced there isn't a serial killer stalking the tube forums, I bring up the video from last night. I watch it again from the beginning. I'm more convinced than ever that it's from my building, though. That's kinda hot. These people went to extremes. The video is almost production quality. Looks like they used a real video camera and not just a cell phone. I notice something weird with the angle. It looks like it was taken by a third person, someone standing in one of the stalls. It shakes once in a while so I doubt the camera is on a tripod. But whoever is holding the camera doesn't show up in the mirror. That's mildly disturbing, like the person chose their location very specifically so as not to be seen.

I scroll through the comments until I see the weird one again.

"I warned you."

Username is Matt Elliott. I click on his name and it brings me to his profile. Most of the fields are blank but he has a picture there. Odds are pretty good it's not actually him unless he's a dead ringer for a young Ryan Gosling. I see a list of videos he's added himself and ones he's liked. Huh. It shows he "liked" one of my early videos. Looks like Mr. Elliot's added a few personal exhibitionist videos as well. I click on the first one and glance at my watch.

"Shit!" I have to leave that instant or I'm going to be late for work. Matt Elliott will have to wait.

I lose myself in the zombie horde heading into the subway underground. The coffee I grabbed from Timmies isn't working fast enough. Once I've lined up in the station to wait for the train, I read news on my phone. Usually, the connection is shoddy, but today I actually get a signal. Still no new real information on the murders but lots of speculation. Editorializing. Gay rights activists are using the string of deaths to expose dangers LGBT youth experience daily. Another article criticizes the police force as inherently homophobic dating back to the bathhouse raids of the 1980s.

Of course, I don't actually read these articles. I just skim the headlines because I really don't care about the murders. It's pure sensationalism. Anyone who can read knows rates of violent crime have been decreasing for decades. But that fact doesn't sell newspapers. Like anyone actually buys newspapers anymore.

The zombie horde boards the train. I've lost my connection so I'm playing Sudoku on my phone when I get this strange feeling. My fight/flight response kicks into overdrive, which is either the start of a panic attack or the feeling that something around me is off. I lift my eyes and scan the crowd. The feeling grows stronger, like my eyes are seeing something that shouldn't be there, but I can't figure out what it is.

Like I said, this is part of my disorder: the constant anxiety that things are not where they are supposed to be, and if I can just get them back where they belong I'll be safe again. The universe is supposed to be orderly, and when it's not, I go a little bit crazy.

So I'm sitting there feeling this panic spread through me, and I want to run away. But I don't see anything I should actually be afraid of. No one is looking at me. And it's not like I see a masked man in the corner of my eye holding a knife. But I feel like there's one.

One of these people is the killer.

I know this is a crazy thought, but I can't ignore it. They always say you should listen to your gut, but what if your gut is flawed? I'm in a near-constant state of fight or flight. But I'm stuck until the next station and there's nothing to fight. So instead . . . panic attack.

I clench and unclench my fists. Slow breaths. My ears start to itch and my head swims like I'm on an elevator that's going down too quickly.

"I have to get out of here." I'm four stops from work. I'll never make it that long. The creepy robot-woman's voice comes over the P.A. system announcing we've arrived at Chester Station. I bolt. I push my way through the horde and run. I take a second to look back only when I'm halfway up the stairs to the surface. No one is following me.

I look through the windows of the train. A muscular man with short strawberry-blond hair looks in my direction. He smiles.

I know it's probably nothing. As the train pulls away, I think of dozens of rational explanations. Odds are the man never even saw me. He was probably zoned out listening to music or daydreaming. I head back down and wait for the next train. The panic is gone but there's a new feeling now.

That man.

There was something about him.

"I know him," I say aloud. "Where do I know him from?"

∗∗∗∗

I'm ten minutes late for work. No one notices, but I have to clock in, so I know my pay will be docked. I sign onto my computer and log into the phone queue. After that, my brain stops working.

I haven't always been like this. Back when I was a kid, I used to be normal. Shy, but normal. I used to smile. I remember that. Well, actually I don't remember anything, but I've seen the pictures. Me holding a big inflated ball standing on a beach. Me climbing a slide. Me blowing out candles surrounded by family. In all these pictures, I'm smiling. I see these pictures in my mind, and I try not to feel bitter. But that boy died when I was twelve. He was murdered. The police rescued my body. It survived, but the boy I was did not.

My parents didn't put me into therapy right away. Don't judge them. It wouldn't have done any good. It took me years to recognize how broken I was. Even if I'd gone to a shrink the second after they found me, I honestly don't think it would have helped. They say kids' brains don't fully develop until they're nearly twenty. That's one explanation. Or maybe I was just doing an excellent job pretending I had amnesia.

Even though I never talk about it, I still recall every second of my time in that basement. I close my eyes and I'm back there again.

Sometimes at night, when the lights are out, I still hear his panting, smell the stench of his week-old sweat. I hear the slap of his flesh against mine and the cries of the others. My memory for faces is shit, but my memory of the basement is vivid. Which makes sleeping difficult sometimes. What I wouldn't give to forget. The ones with repressed memories, they're the lucky ones. All my wounds are just below the surface.

***

It's lunch time, and I'm sitting in the food court on the main floor of my building. Outside, a gentle snow falls. Inside, the food court is full, but no one sees me. Everyone has their eyes fixated on their phones or the person next to them. I could strip naked and jerk off right here and no one would notice.

A part of me wants to test that theory, but I'm not that far gone yet. My workplace is off limits.

Kevin slides through the revolving door and heads towards me. He holds two brown paper bags, one in each hand. He sees me, and his eyes light up.

At least one person in the world sees me.

"Sorry I'm late," he says. Kevin passes me one of the bags.

I smile as I unwrap my gyro. "Strange how you're always late when it's your turn to buy lunch."

"Lies and blasphemy." He points outside. A crowd of reporters and TV cameras encircle the building. "What's up with that?"

I groan and shrug. "Same old thing. My bank is under investigation again because of the whole temporary foreign worker thing. They keep trying to get employees to comment on the situation . . . as if anyone could be stupid enough to do that."

Kevin unwraps his own gyro and takes a bite. "Why doesn't security get rid of them?"

I roll my eyes. "They do. Ten minutes later, there's a new crew. Why are reporters such jerks?"

Kevin opens his mouth to say something, but shakes his head and takes another bite. Silently, he eats his gyro, and I'm grateful. I'm aware that I'm projecting again. I don't hate these reporters. They just trigger something in me. Memories of when I was younger and the vulture reporters that descended on my family after the cops rescued me. Kevin knows and lets the comment go.

Have I mentioned how awesome Kevin is?

We talk about sports for a bit and I tell him about Tonia.

"What about you?" I ask. "How are things going with that new girl you're seeing?"

Kevin wipes his mouth with a napkin. "Which girl?"

"So you've got several on the go again? The one with the crazy stalker eyes from the club. You keep sending me pics of her."

Kevin blinks slowly. "You mean Melissa? I haven't seen her since that night. She's hardly my girl."

I let it drop. I know Kevin. Once he's done with a girl, it's like they never existed.

We finish lunch and Kevin stands. "Ready for beers tonight?"

"Hell, yeah," I say. Kevin and I go for beers with a gang of guys a few times a month. I know most of them from my disastrous one year at Humber College. A few others are from work. Suddenly a beer sounds like the best thing ever. "Are you heading there right after work?"

A strange expression passes over Kevin's face and he looks away.

I frown.

Kevin laughs and runs a hand over his face. "Sorry. Just a work thing I got going on."

"Really?" Now I'm interested. Kevin never talks about work. Like ever. I've started to wonder if he secretly works for the CIA or something instead of a law firm. He's just a clerk but he makes way more money than I do.

Kevin sits back down and leans toward me. "It's the weirdest thing, Clive. I found this weird file with reports and graphs called Guangzho. And before you ask, no it is not a kung fu movie. Guangzho is a major industrial city in China.

"I knew that," I say.

Kevin lowers his head and gives me this look like it's completely impossible for me to know this.

"I'm serious," I say. "You know my dad worked in China when I was in high school. That's back when he still acknowledged I exist. Guangzho was the last place he worked before coming back to Canada. Remember, that's when my mom was convinced he had a new girlfriend because he stopped sending support checks?"

Kevin's eyes go narrow for a second. "Yeah. I completely forgot about that. Anyway, I'm looking at these reports about an industrial accident, some sort of explosion at a plastics factory last year. Only it didn't make sense because I can't tell if we're defending the corporation or helping the families of the people killed in the blast."

I nod and try to look like I'm still interested. This is way more boring than I expected.

Kevin looks over his shoulder then leans in even closer. "So I print off a few things and take them to my boss and he gets super freaked. He grabs the reports from my hands and gets all red in the face. He starts blubbering like an idiot but only for a second. Then he gets super calm. He tells me he'll take care of it."

"Huh," I say. "That is a little suspicious. Kind of John Grisham-y."

"Ya think? But that's not the weird part. I went into work today and my boss is gone. Completely gone like he never existed. His office is empty. I mean, there's not even any furniture and the carpet looks freshly steam-cleaned. I asked what happened to him. No one knows."

My OCD is excellent at spotting things that don't belong. Something about Kevin's story makes me nervous, and I suddenly need to be somewhere safe. But I know I have to comfort Kevin. So I just smile. "And what? You're worried you'll be next? You watch too many movies."

Kevin looks over his shoulder and sighs. "You're probably right. I should be getting back." He stands up again and fist bumps me. "I'll see you at the pub later."

Before I can say anything else, Kevin walks away. I feel like a crappy friend.

CHAPTER SIX

I end up getting back from lunch five minutes late. Delilah meets me by the time clock and winks, stopping me before I punch back in.

"You didn't," I say.

She puts a finger to her lips and shushes me. "I don't know what you're talking about, Clive Dufault. I would never punch in for you because I noticed you were running late."

I want to kiss her, just a peck on the cheek, but I know I can't do that. Delilah laughs, and warmth rushes through my face. Damn. Am I blushing?

The rest of my day is filled with horrendous, vile customers who need therapy much more than I do. But that's why the company pays me the big bucks, right? I take deep breaths, patiently solve their problems, fix their statements, and try to up-sell credit cards and financial investments. It's a living.

I rush home to change before heading out to meet Kevin and the gang. I turn the key to my door.

No click.

I freeze. For a second I can't breathe. Was there really no click? Maybe there was one and I just didn't hear it. A normal person would just open the door, check inside. Worst-case scenario, I didn't lock the door. The odds are pretty small anyone would have even noticed. It's a secure building with security monitoring the main entrance twenty-four-seven. Without a key, you have to be buzzed in.

I can't move. I stare at the doorknob and take my hand off the keys, leaving them in the lock. I listen, but all I hear is the hum of the elevator moving between floors. I press my ear to the door, which is stupid. It's a fire door and does an amazing job of blocking out noise from the hallway. That and concrete walls keep down noise complaints between apartments. I back away and sit on the carpeted floor, staring at my keys.

I don't know what to do.

I hear a voice. "Clive? What's wrong?"

It's Amy. She's walking towards me with that guy from the laundry room. I must look like an idiot, so I get up.

"Nothing," I say. "Just a tough day. Who's your friend?"

The guy rolls his eyes. "Christ. I'm Gabriel. I've lived next to you for like two years, Clive. Amy has introduced us at least ten times."

I wince. "Yikes. Sorry, dude. My bad."

Amy and the guy I suppose is my neighbor, Gabriel, walk to the front door of the apartment next to mine. Amy looks over at me as Gabriel unlocks the door to his apartment. She's probably wondering why I'm still in the hallway. Normal people don't sit in hallways because they're afraid to enter their apartments. Amy frowns, watching me.

Damn it. I turn the knob and push my apartment door open. Before I can think about it, I take my key out of the lock, step inside, and close the door.

Silence. The fridge clicks a little and the fan inside my computer whirls. I leave the door unlocked in case I have to make a fast retreat. I search the apartment, room by room.

Of course, I find nothing. No one is waiting for me inside. Everything is exactly as I left it this morning.

"Must have forgot to lock it this morning. That happens to normal people all the time. I was so tired this morning I'm surprised I remembered to put on shoes. Get it together, Clive."

Still, I don't want to be alone in my apartment any longer than I have to. I don't even bother to change. I pop some valerian root, grab a jacket, and head out. In the hallway, I lock the door and stop. I unlock it. The click is loud. I open the door, close it, and relock it. Just to be sure.

***

There's almost twenty friends in our group at the bar. Some of them, I like. Some annoy the hell out of me. But at least Kevin's there, so it's all good. They're all into their second or third drink by the time I show up. The talk is loud. Everyone's happy to see me. Several buy me shots, so I know tomorrow morning is going to be another rough one. Everything is going swell until she walks in.

Delilah.

Her hair is pulled back and she has a bit more makeup on than usual. Beside her is some annoyingly-attractive man I don't recognize. He's a little older than her with dark Italian good looks and crisp black clothing. I hate him immediately. The jerk whispers something in her ear and Delilah smiles. She looks over, sees me, and the smile drops from her face. For some reason, she looks guilty.

"You know her?" Kevin asks

I shrug. "Kinda. Her name's Delilah. We work together."

"Hmm. I see." Kevin gives me this look like he doesn't really believe what I'm saying.

"Nothing to see." I glance at him.

He raises an eyebrow.

"Stop it. I'm serious. There's nothing going on." I go back to looking at Delilah, who keeps smiling whenever the annoyingly-attractive Italian guy talks.

"Who are we scoping out?" This comes from Kevin's brother, Jay. He's a jerk.

"We're not scoping anyone." I turn away from Delilah and finish my beer.

Jay grunts. "Seriously. You're into her?"

Kevin hits Jay in the arm. "Zip it."

Jay hits Kevin back. "I'm just saying, if she's your thing you won't have much competition."

"What do you mean?" I wave to the waitress for another beer.

"We are looking at the same woman, right? The chubby one with the double—"

"Enough!" Kevin interrupts. "Go be an idiot somewhere else."

Jay laughs, holds his hands up in surrender and walks away.

Like I said, he's a jerk.

"Ignore him," Kevin says. "Does she know you're in to her?"

"I'm not . . ." I stop speaking when I see Kevin's giving me that look again. The one that says I'm being stupid. He's one of the few people that knows about the incident in my childhood and how bad my OCD is. I glance back at Delilah. She's sitting alone at a table. Her date is over by the bar ordering drinks. "I work with her, man. I can't allow myself to be into her. You know my track record."

"I also know it's crazy easy to find a call center job in this city. If you could see the expression on your face when she walked in here with another man . . . I'm just saying, maybe she's worth finding a new job."

Hmm. I hadn't thought about that. Which means I'm basically an idiot.

I know that Delilah has seen me. What a normal person would do is wave at her and go say hi. I should introduce myself to her date just to make sure he is a date and not her brother or something. But before I can head over, the Italian-looking guy is back with drinks. He says something to her and Delilah laughs again. I don't want to ruin their thing, so I focus on drinking instead.

Soon I've had so many shots I barely know where I am. This leads to massive vomiting. Before I know it, I'm in a cab with Kevin. He's taking me back to my apartment. I wave at the security guard as he buzzes us in. It's not the first time he's seen me like this. I don't really remember the ride up the elevator, but I come around when we stop in front of my door.

"Key." Kevin says.

I reach in my pocket and take out my keys. "She's beautiful, isn't she?"

Kevin nods as he unlocks the door. "My advice? Tell her how you feel before it's too late. Take a risk, dude."

He helps me into my bedroom and takes off my shoes.

"Mind if I crash on the couch?" Kevin asks.

"Fuck if I care." The room is spinning, and I feel like I'm falling into a great big hole. A thought forms in my head: did I hear a click when the door opened? Did Kevin even lock the door behind him?

I'm too drunk to get up and check. I try to blink but my eyes refuse to reopen, so I guess I pass out.

CHAPTER SEVEN

My alarm goes off and I want to punch the world. Instead, I take a really long, cold shower. Halfway through washing my hair, I remember that Kevin crashed on my couch last night. I get out of the shower and wrap a towel around my waist.

"Kevin? Get up. We'll be late for work."

No response.

I scrub my hands through my hair to help it dry and walk into the living room. He's not on the couch but his phone's there on the coffee table.

"Kevin?"

Silence. I walk past the front door. It's locked, deadbolt in place. I check the bedroom and the balcony. No sign of him.

"Weird." I double check the time on his phone to make sure I didn't sleep in. Nope. It's 6:30 in the morning, Wednesday. Maybe Kevin woke up in the middle of the night and took a cab home. Strange he left his phone, though. And how would he have locked the door behind him? Part of me is starting to panic, which is stupid. It's not like the serial killer broke into my house last night, kidnapped Kevin, and locked the door behind him.

I get dressed and eat some cereal, thinking maybe Kevin will show up or at least call. I remember his phone's here. Maybe he'll call me from work. I grab his cell phone just in case. If he calls me later in the day, I can drop it by his place.

I run to catch the bus because I don't want to be late again. It's snowing, much harder than yesterday. That and the cold air are not doing any wonders for my hangover.

When I get to work, Delilah is waiting for me by the elevator. Crap. I grin, give her a little wave and try to act normal. I don't think it's working. She's looking at me with this intense expression on her face. That's the "we need to talk" look. But I don't want to talk, not here in this crowded lobby. I don't even know what I would say.

"You look like crap," she says. She reaches over and brushes hair away from my forehead. I look into her eyes and suddenly the lobby doesn't seem that crowded. She takes her hand away hesitantly as the elevator door opens. Neither one of us makes a move to go upstairs. When the elevator leaves, the silence is a little uncomfortable, so I say something stupid.

"So did you have a good time last night?"

Delilah turns away and frowns. "Sorta. I guess. I just met Jeremy and—"

"You don't owe me any explanations." Oops. I said that a little too quickly. I close my eyes and take a breath. "I mean it's not like we're . . ."

Delilah leans over quickly and gives me a peck on the cheek. "You're an idiot." She walks away. I have no idea where she's going or why she did that. If she thinks I'm an idiot, why did she just kiss me? And if she wanted to kiss me, why is she crying? I swear it's like women are a completely different species.

By lunch time I still haven't heard from Kevin. The alarm bells in my head grow louder, so I try calling him at work. The receptionist tells me he called in sick. I ask if she actually talked to him and realize immediately the question sounds kind of odd. She tells me no. He emailed in to say he wasn't feeling well. It should make me relax but it doesn't. I think back to the story of his boss disappearing and that takes my mind to all sorts of fun places. Of course I know I'm just overreacting. Drunk people make bad decisions. He probably couldn't sleep on my couch and decided to go home. Because he was drunk, he forgot his phone. It's logical. Still, I send him a message on Facebook letting him know I have his phone, and I'll drop it by his place after work.

I'm eating in the lunchroom when Delilah walks in. For a second she just looks at me, like she wants to say something, but she leaves.

Ah, man. Usually I have to actually date girls before things get weird between us. This is the part where I'm supposed to chase after her. I think women like that sort of thing, right? But how do I know if I'm being romantic or a stalker?

"Screw it." I throw the rest of my lunch in the garbage and follow her. She's halfway down the hallway but, for the moment, we're alone. "Delilah. Wait."

She stops but doesn't turn around to look at me. "What?"

"How long have we worked together? Two years?"

She nods but doesn't turn around.

"Please don't let things get weird between us. I like you. Probably more than I should, and if this Jeremy guy makes you happy, I'm good with that." I walk towards her. I can feel my face flush. It's like I'm on fire and I find it hard to speak. "But if he doesn't, if . . ." I look at my hands. They're shaking a little. "I'd like to get to know you better. I think you and me could be something even though I'm a complete mess and I'll probably just screw things up. Maybe you'll end up hating me, but I think you're pretty amazing, and I'd be willing to take the risk. So are you interested?"

Whoa. I can't believe I actually said that. Kevin would be proud.

Delilah turns back. I don't know what I was expecting but it wasn't this. She looks angry. She walks up to me, punches me in the chest, and hugs me. She's crying again. She walks away. When she gets to the end of the hallway, she stops and turns back to me. She smiles, nodding.

I'm so confused. "Is that a yes?"

Delilah laughs.

I still don't know if that was a yes.

When I get back to my desk, my phone buzzes. It's a message on Facebook from Kevin. He says he's still hung over and wants me to drop the phone off at his place after work. See. He's not dead. No serial killer drama. John Grisham would be disappointed. Looks like today's turning out to be okay after all.

***

I take the subway to Kevin's place. He lives in a pretty sketchy part of town because he's trying to save up money for a down payment on a condo. There's no security in his building, so no one has to buzz me in. I walk up to the third floor and ring his doorbell.

No answer.

I wait for a bit and ring again.

"Wake up, Kevin. Answer the damn door."

No answer.

After waiting a bit longer, I decided to try the doorknob. Maybe he left it open and he's in the bathroom or something. It's not locked, so I push the door open and go inside.

The first thing I notice is the blood.

Not much. Just a few drops. I jump back into the hallway. Instant panic attack.

"Get it together, Clive." I slap my face a few times. I stare through the open door at the drops of blood on the white carpet. There are dozens of rational reasons why it's there. Kevin used to get nose bleeds in high school. Maybe it's not even blood. Sure, it looks like it but I'm not a forensic expert. It could be anything.

"Kevin? Are you here?" I call out his name as I step back inside the apartment. No response. My heart's pounding and I try to talk myself down. "You're overreacting, Clive. If Kevin's hurt, he may need your help."

I see the overturned furniture. His apartment has been trashed. Cushions ripped apart. Mirrors smashed. I see the shirt Kevin wore last night folded neatly on the kitchen table. Beside it are Kevin's shoes and, of all things, a Lillie doll. It's like a Barbie doll, but cheaper.

"What the fuck?" I'm shaking now, and it feels like bugs are crawling over my skin as I check out the rest of the apartment. There's no sign of Kevin.

I run back out to the hallway and start pacing. What do I do? Maybe there's a rational reason for this, but I can't think of one. So I take my phone out and dial 911.

It takes the cops almost an hour to get there. I'm kind of surprised when they show up because they aren't in uniform. They show me badges, but seriously, how the hell would I know if they're real or not? I haven't seen a badge since I was a kid. There are two of them, a white man with dark brown hair and a huge gut and a trim Chinese woman with short black hair. They tell me their names, but I immediately forget them.

I tell them about the last time I saw Kevin, how he left my apartment, and the last message he sent me. When I tell them about finding Kevin's shirt and the freakin' Lillie doll, the man's expression slips. It's just for a second but I can tell the doll means something to him. He glances at the woman, but she doesn't look back at him. Instead, she steps into the apartment, kneels down in front of the blood and shakes her head. She takes out her phone and makes a call. I think I hear her call for the CSI squad or something, but she's talking in a whisper. I give them the names and numbers of Kevin's family. The male detective asks if they can take

Kevin's phone. I feel weird about it, but I pass the phone to him. Maybe they can run a trace on the last number he called or something. I've seen them do things like that before on TV.

"It's probably nothing to worry about," the man cop says. "You said your friend was drunk. Maybe he tossed the apartment himself."

I shake my head, insulted. "Because anyone ever does that."

The officer sighed. "People do all sorts of things when they've had too much to drink."

The female cop comes out of the apartment typing notes on her phone. She looks at her partner and nods once. She heads back inside and uses her phone to take pictures of the room.

"Listen," the guy says as he's scribbling in his notepad. "I'm going to ask a sensitive question. I hope you don't get offended, but it could help our investigation. Were you and Kevin . . ."

He lets his voice drop off and I get what he's implying.

"No. He's my friend, dude. Nothing more." The blood drains from my face and my knees wobble. Because I know why he's asking. "Wait. You don't think . . ."

I lean against the wall. Suddenly, I feel too weak to stand.

The detective raises his hands to calm me down. "Let's not jump to conclusions, okay? Like I said, this is likely nothing. If your friend Kevin wasn't gay . . ."

"Please." I feel like I've been punched in the gut. "Please don't use the past tense."

The office shakes his head. "Shit. Sorry. If he isn't gay, he doesn't fit the profile. As I'm sure you can imagine, we've been paying special attention to incidents involving young men lately. How well did you know him?"

I bite my thumbnail. He did the past tense thing again. "I've known him for more than ten years. We grew up together. Moved into the city together. If Kevin was gay, I would know."

The woman comes back out the apartment. I see she's wearing blue latex gloves now and holding her phone out to me. She shows me a picture of Kevin's shirt. "And this is what he was wearing the last time you saw him?"

I nod. My head is spinning.

"Mr. Dufault?" The male officer is waving his notepad in front of my face. I wonder how long I've zoned out for.

"Sorry." I put my head in my hands. The world is heavy and dark. "What can I do?"

The male officer – I really wish I remembered his name – puts his notepad away. "My partner is going to stay here. We have people on the way that will go over your friend's apartment looking for clues. Someone will call his family and friends. Most likely one of them will know where Kevin is. But if not . . . Do you mind if we go to your place?"

I frown. "Why?"

He shrugs. "Maybe nothing. But it's possible that's the last place anyone actually saw Kevin. I'd like to check your apartment, ask around the building and see if anyone saw him leave."

Yep. Very familiar. "You have to clear me as a suspect, right? Try to establish a time line. That's what you do in cases like this."

He gives me a strange look, something I can't interpret. "Yeah. Nothing personal. Tell me, Clive, can you think of anyone who would want to hurt Kevin?"

I think of the thing with his boss. But that's just crazy, so I shake my head. "Everyone loves Kevin. I have no idea what's happening here."

"Are you okay, son?" He lifts his chin. "I know this can be a lot to take in. Odds are there's a boring reason for your friend's disappearance."

"That's what they always say." I close my eyes. "Look, I don't know if you'll find out when you run my name or not. Maybe it's sealed because I was a minor and it has nothing to do with this case but . . . I had an . . . incident when I was a kid."

He's frowning now, and he doesn't look so friendly. "What kind of incident? Did you hurt someone?"

"No." I shake my head. My mouth is super dry, and I can't look him in the eyes. I don't want to see the expression on his face when I tell him. "I was . . . taken. By a man. Only for a few days and the guy is in jail now. So, like I said, it has nothing to do with Kevin, but this whole thing has me completely freaked out. It's triggering all this stuff in me, and I honestly don't know how to deal."

"Fuck." The officer sighs and hangs his head. "I'm sorry, son. Thanks for telling me. We'll make this as quick and painless as possible. Okay?"

I nod and follow him to his car.

I'm barely aware of the city passing by as he drives me back to my apartment in Thornhill. My mind is going to some very dark places, and I'm not sure how to get it back. The detective talks to me as he drives, but I have no idea what he's saying. I nod once in a while, but all I can think about is Kevin.

We stop and talk to the security guard at the front door first. The detective shows his badge and asks some questions. The guard looks at me and says he recognizes me but, since he wasn't working last night, can't confirm when I came home. The cop asks to see the security tapes for the last twenty-four hours. The security guard makes a phone call and a few minutes later the two of them leave to go watch the tapes. While they're gone, I sit on a couch in the front lobby and stare at the floor.

I start second guessing myself. When I woke up this morning and Kevin was gone, my gut told me something was wrong, just like now my gut is telling me Kevin is dead. It tells me I should have gone over to Kevin's place immediately, skipped work and tracked down my friend. Logically, I know my gut lies. It's part of my condition, something I refuse to call a disease. I don't have cancer. I have a cognitive disorder. And one day I'll be strong enough to get my head together. Today is not that day. Today, my best friend is missing, and I would give anything for a magic pill to make this all better.

The elevator dings and I look up as the doors open with a soft whoosh. Amy comes off the elevator with that guy, Gabriel, who I suppose is my next-door neighbor. She waves at me and smiles. The smile drops from her face, and she rushes over to me.

"What's wrong?" she asks.

Before I can say anything, the detective comes out with the security guard. He doesn't look happy.

I stand up, hands in my pockets. "Did you find something?"

The detective shakes his head. "He didn't come out the front door." He glances over at Amy and Gabriel. "Do you know these people?"

Amy extends her hand in introduction. "I'm Amy Vitalli. This is Gabriel Wainwright. We both live here. Is there a problem, officer?"

"We're trying to find this young man's friend, Kevin Nielson. Last seen in this building. Do you know him?"

Amy and Gabriel shake their heads.

My phone buzzes with a Facebook notification. I think of checking it in case it's from Kevin but don't want to be rude in front of the officer.

The detective has his notepad out again. "Did either of you hear or see anything out of the ordinary last night or this morning?"

Gabriel clears his throat. "I live in the apartment next to Clive, but the walls are concrete. Pretty soundproof. Though I did hear two voices in the hallway. I think it was around 1:00 last night but I can't be sure."

The Facebook notification pings again.

I nod. "That sounds around about the time we got back here."

Gabriel looks at his watch. "Crap. Amy, we have to go, or this weather will make us late. We have a nine o'clock reservation downtown."

Only then do I realize how late it is. It seems like only a few minutes ago I was leaving work. I look outside through the floor-to-ceiling windows in the lobby, only now noticing how strong the storm is. Snowmageddon is alive and well.

The detective says a few more words, which I'm barely listening to. He gives Gabriel his card in case he thinks of anything later.

My phone rings. I look to the detective and he nods his permission for me to answer the phone. Surprisingly, it's my mother.

"My god," she says. "I can't believe it. Did you see Facebook?"

"I'm kind of busy, Mom," I say. Her voice is soft and haggard. I can tell it's bad news. Probably a great aunt died or something. "Can I . . .?"

"Oh, my poor baby. You haven't seen it yet. Are you sitting down?"

"Can it wait?" I roll my eyes and wave goodbye to Amy and Gabriel.

"No, it can't. It's about your friend Kevin, baby. I think you should sit down."

I pull the phone away from my ear and look at the Facebook notification.

I can hear my mom's voice, still talking to me. I'm vaguely aware that the detective is talking to me, too, but I'm completely disconnected from the world. It's like the only thing that exists is that phone screen. I press the Facebook notification button.

A picture appears on my screen.

I scream and scream and scream. I throw the phone, and I can feel the police officer trying to grab me, to stop me from thrashing, but it doesn't work.

I scream for a very long time.

CHAPTER EIGHT

I'm sitting on a plastic chair in a lounge somewhere. I think it's a police station. A woman comes in to tell me my mother is on her way to pick me up. Someone else hands me a cup of coffee, but I can't bring myself to drink anything.

I hear people talking around me. They say the picture has been removed from Facebook but it's probably too late. Hundreds of people could have seen it by now. There's no way to guarantee it will be taken off the internet. Someone will have screenshot it and it's likely the image will find its way to the media. That's the thing, isn't it? Once you put something online, it's there forever and ever. Just like it will be in my head forever and ever.

Kevin. Topless. His face red and bulging. Strangled with plastic rope, tied to a chain-link gate in what looks like a subway station. They haven't found his body yet. I know it's stupid, but a part of me is still hoping this is all some joke. Like Kevin is trying to get attention or something. But that's not Kevin. He would never do something like this, not to his family and not to me. He knows what I went through.

My throat is killing me from all the screaming and crying. I'm exhausted. Partly – mostly – because my best friend is dead. But also because I know my gut reaction was right. The serial killer took my friend. If I was right about that, what else was I right about? I have to tell someone. The whole ridiculous thing.

I go to reach for my phone before remembering I threw it somewhere. I have no idea what happened to it, and suddenly that seems very important. The door to the lounge opens and the male detective walks in with his female partner.

"How are you doing, Clive?" he asks.

I scoff and stare at my coffee. It's an insulting question.

The woman pulls up a chair and sits directly in front of me. "We're sorry for your loss, Clive, but we need to ask you a few more questions. Do you think you can answer them? If you want a lawyer . . ."

"Jesus fucking Christ." I drop the cup of coffee. I don't throw it. I just take my hands away and let it fall to the floor. Lukewarm coffee splatters the hem of my pants. I'm so mad right now I want to bash her head, but I swallow my rage. "I don't need a fucking lawyer. I didn't do this. I didn't kill my best friend. I know that and so do you. No wonder everyone says you're fucking up this investigation. So can we stop the nonsense and just ask your fucking questions? You know what? Let me ask you a question first. Are you sure that Jerry Tran was a suicide?"

Both cops stare at me blankly.

"Who is Jerry Tran?" the man says.

I lean back and focus on breathing. "He worked in my building. He was found dead a few days ago. I've seen nothing about it in the press, but the rumor is he killed himself. Are you sure?"

The woman goes to the door and motions for someone. I hear her whispering something about files and reports. She comes back.

The male officer is looking at me very closely. "You think this Jerry Tran was murdered? Why?"

So I tell them.

I keep my eyes on the ground as I talk about my videos and the weird comment. I talk about the video I saw with the Asian guy and the woman. I'm surprised I can actually admit all this in public. Probably because I don't really give a shit any more. My inner critic screams at me, saying they can charge me for public indecency or hold me for a psych eval.

"I don't care if you think I'm a pervert," I say. "I never hurt anyone. I'll do anything I can to help you catch this sick bastard."

For a moment, when I stop talking, there is silence. The male officer clears his throat.

"Well," he says. "That was . . . unexpected. You've given us a lot to look into, Clive. Do you have somewhere you can spend the night?"

I look up, confused. "Can't I go home?"

The female officer's eyes go wide. "Are you sure you want to? Look, Mr. Dufault, we don't know yet if Kevin was taken from your apartment or not. But if he was, that means there was someone else inside your apartment. We spoke with your property manager. We're having your locks changed just as a precaution, but that won't get done until morning. If you don't have anywhere else to go, I recommend staying in a hotel."

The image of my front door appears in my head. I think of unlocking the door and not hearing the click. What if the killer had been in my house several times? But that's insane. If the killer had broken into my house, why am I still alive? More importantly, though, was I willing to risk it?

I nod. "Fine. My mom's on her way. I'll go home with her for a few days. You have her number, obviously. Please call if there's anything I can do."

***

It's almost an hour before my mom shows up. She still lives in Brantford, in the house we moved into after Dad left. Even though she got in her car almost immediately after the male police officer – what was his name, anyway? – told her to meet us at the headquarters, traffic can be horrendous along the 403. She hugs me when she shows up, but I pull away. I don't want to break down again, not in public.

You may be wondering where my father is. Me too. He left years ago, not long after my incident. He told me he didn't know how to be my father anymore, didn't know what to say. He said he knew it wasn't my fault and that he was an ass for feeling that way but he could barely look at me anymore. My mom wasn't having any of that nonsense and kicked him out. I haven't seen in him in years.

My mother looks an awful lot like me. Same blond hair, same brown eyes. I have my father's nose and cheekbones, though. She still looks young enough to be my sister.

She places her hand on my cheek and looks me in the eye. "I'm going to talk to the man over there for a second, okay? Then we can go."

I nod and watch as she goes to talk to the police officer. She looks strong, but I can tell from the streaks around her eyes that she's been crying. I can't hear what they talk about, but the officer keeps looking over at me. Each time he does it's like I can hear my father whispering in my ear.

Man up.

Men aren't supposed to cry. Men have to be strong and brave for everyone around them. I was twelve, having nightmares about the man who took me, and my father had no clue how to be supportive. He gave me the only advice he knew how to give.

Man up.

I sit back down on the plastic chair and try to tune out the sounds around me. I start counting the floor tiles, but it doesn't help me relax. I look around and count the number of exits. I see six open doors and three closed ones. Two of the closed doors are fire exits. My ears start to itch, and I try to recall the last time I cleaned them. I think I cleaned them before and after my shower this morning but it's been hours.

I use my pinkie finger but it's too big. I can't get to where it . . .

"Clive." My mother's voice interrupts my thoughts. From the look on her face it isn't the first time she has tried to get my attention. She holds something out for me: a small baggie filled with cotton swabs. I smile, relieved. A moment later I blush, embarrassed.

"Thanks." I take the baggy and put it in my pocket. "I'll be back in a second."

The detective showed me where the bathroom was earlier. I lock myself in and wet one end of a swab. I clean my right ear first. Five circles wet, five circles dry. I always take a new swab for the other ear. I started doing this after the incident. I don't know why it has to be five times or why I have to do the right ear first. All I know is if I don't follow the ritual properly, I'm compelled to do it again. When I'm very stressed, sometimes I clean my ears hourly. I know it's weird, but I'm not hurting anyone, and I've never injured my eardrum or anything. I'm just glad I'm not one of the hand washers. Those people are nuts.

I come back to find my mother holding my phone.

"Thanks," I take it from her. "I was wondering where it was."

"Mr. Coyle collected it for you," she says. "The screen's broken but maybe we can get something off it."

"Who's Mr. Coyle?"

She points over at the male officer. At least now I know his name.

"Oh. Phone's probably toast. These things bust if you sneeze on them the wrong way. I'd like to get some of the pictures off it, though. There were a few of me and . . ." Kevin's face fills my mind. I can't say his name yet. I honestly don't even know how to start processing the fact he's gone. "Have you talked to his mother?"

She shakes her head. "I got in the car as soon as I could. Poor woman. What kind of sick monster puts a picture like that on Facebook where . . ." She takes a deep breath and looks away.

"The world is full of monsters, mom. You know that."

She nods, and I see she's starting to cry again. "Mr. Coyle said you're coming home for a couple of days. Just to be safe."

For a moment I'm paralyzed. I wonder how much Coyle has told her. Did he mention my videos? No. I'm sure my mom would be acting weird around me if she knew about that. I know she loves me, but everyone has limits.

I put my arm around her shoulder. She's almost a foot shorter than me. I try to think of something to say, something to make her not worry, but I can't. Truth is, even in the middle of the police station, I'm completely terrified.

"Can we run by the apartment first? I need to pack a few things. Is Russell here?"

Russell is her boyfriend. Sorry, partner. They've lived together for years now. Thankfully, he's amazing to my mom. You can tell by the way he looks at her that he's completely in love. When I was younger, it made me gag. Now, I realize they are two of the luckiest people on the planet.

"No," Mom says. "He's working the afternoon shift. Won't be home for hours. I called him on the way up, though, told him what happened. He wanted to come with me, but I said there was nothing for him to do. Are you sure it's safe to go back to the apartment? I could always stop by Walmart and buy you a few things."

"It will be fine, Mom." I keep my arm around her shoulders as we walk out of the headquarters. "There's a security guard covering the front door and we'll only be there a few minutes. "I don't want to live my life in fear. It's not healthy."

We head towards the side exit because, apparently, there are news crews at the main entrance. Before we leave, the male officer – Coyle, I guess his name is – waves at me. He wants to speak to me alone for a second.

"Wait here," I tell my mom. I walk over to Coyle and see he's got a green folder in his hands. He opens it and I see pictures and notes, but Coyle's angled them in such a way I can't see any details.

"I wanted to tell you what we looked into Jerry Tran's death." Coyle closes the folder and puts it behind his back. "No evidence of foul play. If there is a connection to the others, we can't see it. But we'll keep looking." He looks over my shoulder at my mother. "As for your . . . extracurricular activities, I'm willing to keep that off the record for now. Promise me you won't make any more videos in public places and—"

"Deal." I interrupt him, feeling waves of embarrassment and relief pass over me. I don't think I could live if Mom knew what I was doing.

He nods and starts to turn away. I take that as my cue to leave.

But the annoying little voice, the one that tells me to check the front door, whispers to me again. It's saying they don't see the connection, but I maybe I could.

I clear my throat. "Did Tran have a tattoo on his back? Peacock feathers with an exaggerate eye?"

Coyle stops. Frowns. "I didn't bother to check. Why?"

"Maybe nothing." I shrug, feeling like a completely loser. I mean why am I even saying this? "It's just I have slight to moderate OCD. I notice things that are out of place. The guy in the video I saw was pretty masculine, but he had this really girly tattoo."

Coyle inhales slowly. "I'll look into it. Do me a favor. Keep your theories on Tran to yourself until we've proven a connection. His family has been through enough."

I narrow my eyes. "He has a family? Like wife and children?"

Coyle puts a hand on my shoulder and turns me around to face my mother. "Go home, Mr. Dufault. You've suffered a great loss. Leave the detective work to the professionals."

I nod and blush, feeling even more stupid now.

But I still want a look at that file.

CHAPTER NINE

Turns out there's no reason for Mom to be nervous going to my apartment. When I get to the lobby, the same security guy that saw my meltdown is there. He tells me there's still a few officers going door to door around the building asking my neighbors if they've seen anything. He also says I just missed the media circus. He says there were several camera crews out in the parking lot less than an hour ago. Which is freaking fantastic. By this time tomorrow the whole building will probably hear about my episode. Guess it's time to find a new apartment.

I unlock my door and stand there for a second. Inside it's dark and quiet but it doesn't really feel like home anymore. I remember sitting in the hallway in a panic because I wasn't sure I'd locked the door. But maybe it wasn't all in my mind. Maybe someone really did break into my place. Who knows what they did in here? And if they did take Kevin when he was passed out on my couch . . .

Mom reaches past me and turns on the light. "I can pack for you."

I shake my head. "No. I got this." I take a deep breath and step inside. I quickly look over at my computer, thanking the gods that my monitor is turned off. My mother definitely does not need to see my porn star wallpaper. Looking in that direction, I'm suddenly hyperaware of the cum stains on my computer seat. The air smells of flatulence and sweat. Everything is filthy.

I know Coyle had officers search my place for clues, but the apartment is nowhere near as messed up as I expected. You've seen how they toss places in the movies. This is nothing like that. A few pieces of furniture out of place. A bit of white powder from what I assume is fingerprint powder.

"Sorry," I saw to my mom. "Wasn't expecting guests. I'll just be a minute."

I head to my bedroom and an unexpected smell hits me. Tonia's perfume. I still haven't changed the sheets. Having sex with her feels like it happened in another life time. I reach into my closet to pull out my overnight bag when another thought hits me.

"What if Kevin really didn't send those pictures?"

I sit on the bed, my mind racing. I pull my phone out of my pocket and try turning it on. No use. I really want to get another glimpse of those pictures Kevin sent of the girl he picked up. I remember thinking it wasn't like him to send nude pictures of a sleeping girl. He wasn't usually perverted, well, not that way, at least. He might have been a whore, but he respected women. And when I confronted him on it, he denied sending the pictures. If I could just look at the pictures again, maybe there would be a clue, something I didn't see the first time.

I hear my mom clear her throat, and it snaps me out of my thoughts.

"Sorry." I jump up and start pulling clothes out of the closet. "I'll be quick."

She comes into my room and starts making my bed. I'd tell her to stop but I've known the woman long enough. Once she sets her mind to doing something, nothing will stop her. So instead, I just hurry up. The sooner we're out of here, the less likely she is to see the used condoms in the bedside garbage.

We leave my bedroom, but not before I throw my iPod nano and sleep headphones into my bag. Something tells me I'm definitely going to need help sleeping tonight. I pack my toothbrush and a carton of cotton swabs from the bathroom. I pop four valerian root pills. The little critic in my mind says to log into my iCloud account to check the pics Kevin sent me. Thankfully, I'm able to push that thought down. I'll check that when my mother isn't looking over my shoulder.

We leave my apartment, and I lock the door. After I hear the click, I pull on it a few times to make sure it's secure. I turn and see Amy and Gabriel walking towards

Gabriel's apartment. Amy goes pale and Gabriel fidgets. He waves at me awkwardly and looks away. He turns to unlock his apartment door, but Amy walks over to talk to me.

"Mom, can you give us a minute?"

She nods, reaches out to take my overnight pack, and walks to the elevator.

"I'm so sorry, Clive," Amy says. She's all doe-eyed and gentle. I can't tell if she's being sincere. For a second, I think she's grinning. She's closer than ever to the tragedy now. What an ass. "We weren't sure what had happened, but we figured it out. You were asking about your friend and now it's all over the news—"

"Fucking fantastic!" I rub my ears. Rage flashes through me. This happens sometimes when I know I've lost complete control of a situation. Of course it's all over the news. Kevin was killed by the gay serial killer. I can only imagine what people are saying. "Look, I'm going away for a bit. Few days. Do you think you can convince Gabriel to watch my place for me?"

She nods. Her eyes go wide for a second. "Listen, I don't know if I should be saying something to the police or not. Maybe it's nothing important, but . . ."

"But what?"

The way she's standing, head cocked to the side, she has that look that says I need to think she's important, that she's the center of the universe or something. I'm sure she's going to try to take ownership of recent events, make it all about her. I'm partially right.

"Remember when I said I didn't know the third victim?" She reaches into her purse and pulls out her cell phone. She flips through photos for a second and then holds the phone out for me. "See that guy? That's him."

I grab the phone and look closely at the picture. "This is the third victim?" It's a guy around my age, brown hair, sitting on a park bench. He's got this stupid big grin on like he's having the time of his life. "Who is he?"

"His name is Ethan Marchese. He works – sorry, worked – as a bartender at a bar on Church street. I used to go there with Gabriel and my other gay friends . . ."

"Wait, Gabriel's gay?"

She rolls her eyes and takes the phone back. "We've had this talk before. You were worried he was going to hit on you. Which he so wouldn't. You're way too young for him."

I try to recall when we've ever talked about Gabriel before. Maybe I'm having early Alzheimer's or something. Why can't I remember anything about that guy? And how can I be too young for him? How old is Gabriel, anyway?

Amy flips back through a few more pictures. "I got these pictures off Facebook. I was stalking my friends' profiles after I told you about the new murder. I didn't think the guy's name was familiar, but something about it bugged me. Then, I found this."

She shows me another picture and I feel a bit numb. It's taken in front of my office building. I don't know any of the people in the picture, but I recognize Ethan Marchese. I'm also pretty sure the person beside him is the first murder victim.

"Where did you get this? Is that Ethan with Michael?"

Amy nods and starts to put the phone away.

I grab her hands. "You have to tell the police about this. They probably don't know there's a connection."

"Of course they'd know," she says defensively. "They're professional detectives or something. Besides, it's not like I can prove anything."

I want to grab her phone and hit her in the head a few times. She has this incredibly important piece of information and isn't telling anyone. This could help find the person who murdered Kevin, and she's just going to sit on it.

"Come on," I turn her around and push her towards the elevator. Gabriel, standing in his doorway, looks bewildered and follows us. We take the elevator to the lobby and ask the security guy to track down the police who are still on site. He picks up the phone to do that, but before he can dial, I see them. They're walking towards their car, two muscular men in uniform. If I'd been a little later, I might have missed them.

I run outside and wave them down. I tell them who I am and point at Amy . . . who looks completely ticked off now. I make her tell them what she's found out. She takes out her phone and shows the pictures. Not long after she starts talking, one of the uniformed guys gets on a cell phone. I hear him use the name Coyle and immediately feel relieved. In the movies, discovering how the victims are connected is always the first step in finding the killer.

We get back into Mom's car. It's a long drive back to her place. The snow is heavier than ever now. All you can see are tiny red taillights of the cars ahead of us. We don't talk much, just listen to the sound of the wiper blades and the low murmur of the radio. Mom picks up burgers at a rest stop. I eat but it all tastes like paper to me.

My momentary relief fades away. Because logic. Everyone in Toronto knows Church Street is the gay village. Is it really so strange that the first victim, Michael, a young gay man, might have known a bartender from of one of the clubs? The first and third victims may have known each other, but I know nothing about the second victim, not even his name. You've probably figured out by now, I'm not so good at remembering people's names . . . unless they're a porn star. And even if there is a connection between the first three murders, I can't see how any of it relates to Kevin.

Or do I?

My inner critic starts to wonder. Is it possible Kevin had a double life? Could he have been gay, and I didn't know it? He was always banging chicks. I've met at least ten women he'd seriously dated since high school. Well, at least what Kevin called serious. More like repeated sexual encounters. Was there a part of Kevin I didn't know?

I think about it for a good long while. In the end I don't buy it. Maybe everyone has a side of them that no one else sees. I know I have mine. But Kevin has been my best friend for years. If he was gay, I really think I would know about it. There has to be another connection. Does it have anything to do with the disappearance of Kevin's boss? And only then does it hit me. I've completely dropped the ball. I got angry at Amy for withholding important evidence, and I did the same goddamn thing. I should have told Coyle all about that. But aren't police supposed to ask that type of question? I'm being an idiot. Of course, they ask that question. I'm sure they'll interview everyone at Kevin's work looking for clues, but they aren't going to keep me apprised of their entire investigation. Still, I make a mental note to call Coyle in the morning and tell him about it.

There's also the big question, the one I'm doing a fine job of not thinking about.

Kevin was found in a maintenance area in a subway station. What happened to him between the time he was taking off my shoes in my apartment and the time of his death? Was he taken away forcibly? If so, that means someone was in my apartment. If Kevin left willingly, that suggested he knew the killer. Or killers.

And if Kevin knows him, most likely I do, too.

CHAPTER TEN

"We're here." Mom turns off the ignition. "Home sweet home."

The house is dark, but I hear barking coming from inside. That makes me smile.

"Eddy." I grab my stuff from the back seat, get out of the car, and go to the front bay window. Inside the house, a small Jack Russell terrier is bouncing up and down on the back of a couch, barking hysterically at the window. I tap the glass to tease him. "Good to see you too, little buddy. How's his hip doing, mom?"

My mother unlocks the front door. "Better since he's been on those pills. Your old room's a mess. I've been using it to store my paintings. Give me a few minutes to clean it up. There's beer in the fridge. I'm guessing you could use one."

"Obviously."

As soon as I step inside, Eddy is running around my feet. He bites the hem of my pant leg and pulls. I drop my overnight bag and laugh as I bend down to pet him. He snarls, runs away for a sec and stops. He looks up at me with these eyes that seem too big for his head. I put my hand out to pet him. He walks over, licks my hand once and runs away, barking up a storm.

It feels great to be home until I remember the front door isn't locked. Panic sweeps over me and I slam the door shut. I lock the doorknob and the deadbolt and put the chain in place. I race to the back door and make sure it's locked. I look out the window into the backyard. Nothing moves except the blowing snow and trees swaying in the wind.

I take a deep breath and head to the kitchen.

Mom's standing there, arms crossed. "You stopped taking your medication again, didn't you?"

I groan and grab a beer out of the fridge. "Can we please not have this conversation again?"

"Is it the cost? I don't have much money, but you know I—"

"It's never been about money." I twist off the beer cap and put it in my pocket. "You don't know what those pills do to me. Besides, the doctor said my OCD is manageable. The pills help, but—"

"I'm only suggesting that, with everything that's happened, it might be a good idea to have some pills available. I remember the last time things got really bad, and I don't want—"

"I'll be fine, Mom." I walk over and kiss her on the top of the head. "Promise. If I start drawing on the wall in crayon or seeing dead people, I give you permission to have me committed. Okay?"

She frowns. "Not funny, Mr. Man. If you're still hungry there's leftover roast in the fridge."

When she leaves, I rummage through my overnight bag for the bottle of valerian root. I swallow another four pills with a long swig of beer. Part of me knows she's right. Maybe I should go back on the medication for a bit.

I also remember the last time things got bad.

***

I wake up the next day, Thursday, to the sound of a phone ringing. Eyes still closed, I reach out to answer my cell. I remember what happened to my cell and my eyes flash open.

The phone's still ringing.

I call out for my mom, but she doesn't answer. Dressed in jogging pants and an old t-shirt, I leave my old bedroom and head for the kitchen. They actually still have a home phone and it's actually hung on the wall. What is this, the 1980s?

I answer and hear my mother's voice.

"Were you still sleeping?" she asks.

"No," I lie. "What time is it, anyway?"

"After two o'clock. Russell and I are leaving work early to do some grocery shopping. We'll be home in an hour or so. Do you need anything?"

I hear my dad's voice again. Man up.

"Nope. I'm fine. Well, as fine as I can be." I hesitate for a moment before saying, "Do you think I should call Kevin's mom? Or is it too soon?"

"I honestly don't know. When everything happened with you all those years ago, everyone called. Seems like I spent the entire first day on the phone being polite to people who just wanted to help. Give her a few days. She probably hasn't even made funeral arrangements yet. Poor girl."

When I hang up, I feel like grabbing a beer and crawling into a dark place and staying there. But I hear the voice again.

Man up.

So instead, I make sure the doors are locked and take a shower. I know what I have to do: take control of the situation. I have to stop being a victim. Somehow Kevin caught the attention of a serial killer. I want . . . no I need to know how. So I go onto my mom's computer and started researching.

This is the joy of Google. Almost anything you could ever want to know is searchable data. Kevin's death is big news now, in Canada and around the world. Nothing sells papers quite like fear. And Canada is a country nearing hysteria.

I see pictures of the first victim, Michael Needs. He was a nineteen-year-old college student at U of T. Brown hair, green eyes, lived on campus. They found him in his dorm room, strangled by plastic rope, tied to a chair that faced an open window. Second victim, Fred Dimmerman, twenty-three, was from Scarborough. He worked in a comic book store. As I learned yesterday, the third victim was Ethan Marchese, twenty-two-year-old bartender. Nothing I read online suggests there's a relationship between any of the victims except all were gay white men. But there must be something I'm missing.

When I was a teenager, I went through a phase where I was obsessed with serial killers. I read tons of books and watched a gazillion movies, trying to get inside their minds. I figured if I understood them, maybe it would help me deal with what had happened to me. Sucky part is, it didn't help in the slightest, but I learned how sick minds operate. Everything I know about serial killers suggests these murders aren't random. The victims were chosen for a very specific purpose. Perhaps sexual encounters gone wrong or a crazed religious fanatic committing hate crimes. Sure, I can't see the pattern now, but I know it's there. And if there's one thing I'm good at, it's finding a pattern.

"How are they connected?"

My gut still tells me Jerry Tran is connected. I Google him again and find his obituary. Like Coyle said, Tran had a wife and three children. He is nowhere near the profile for this killer. Looking at his picture I can't really tell if he was the guy from the video I saw. I think about pulling up the video on my mom's computer, but . . . gross. I can't watch porn in her house. I'm not a teenager anymore. I print off his picture, fold it up, and put it in my pocket. I'll try to compare it with the video first chance I get.

I log into my iCloud account and click on photos. There they are: the three pictures Kevin – or someone – sent me of the girl he picked up at the bar. I saved them. Of course, I saved them. I think I mentioned my porn collection is rather extensive. It's not the girl with crazy stalker eyes. In fact, I don't recall seeing her at the club, Cube. She has high cheekbones and long straight black hair. My guess is she's Mohawk like Kevin's father.

Aaaand I never mentioned the pictures to Coyle, either. Damn. What is wrong with my brain?

I save the pictures to my mom's desktop and open them with her default graphics program. She only has Microsoft Paint installed so my options with the pictures are pretty limited. I play with the brightness and contrast, hoping I can catch sight of the picture taker in a reflection somewhere. Nothing. I also look for proof that Kevin was there, but the photos are immaculate. Nothing out of place at all. Still, I print those pictures as well and delete the copies from my mom's desktop. I empty the recycle bin to double ensure my mom never has to see them.

I take the printed pictures to my room and stare at them, searching for something that doesn't belong.

The front door rattles, like someone is trying to unlock it.

I ignore it at first, expecting it to be Mom and Russell. But it hasn't even been an hour since they called. No way they're home already.

So who's on the other side of the door?

I stash the photos beneath my pillow and head to the living room. Eddy is a crappy watch dog. He glances at me and back at the door before falling back asleep. No treats for him today.

The front door has a piece of frosted glass in the middle. I can see there's someone on the other side but they are only a shadow. No way to determine who it is.

"Mom? Is that you?"

The figure stops playing with the lock. I hear it mumble something. I'm pretty sure it's a guy. The figure slips away.

Everything is silent except the clicking of the clock. The longer I stand staring at the frosted glass, the more freaked out I get. I snap out of it and run to the door, checking that it's still locked. I race to the backdoor. Still secure. I go through the entire house, looking out each window. Nothing. Whoever was here is gone now.

So, what do I do? Call the police? What would I tell them? Someone came to my door and left? That's hardly a crime. I know what I'm not going to do. Open the door and check if he is still there. Only idiots do that. I go to the kitchen and find the largest knife I can, sit in the living room, and wait.

Later, I hear a car pull up. I run to the bay window and check outside. When I see Mom and Russell get out of the car, I run back to the kitchen and put the knife away. No reason for them to freak out.

Mom opens the door and I force a smile on my face. As I help her and Russell put groceries away, all I can think about is this – who cares if the door is locked when it's so easy to break a window?

CHAPTER ELEVEN

During super, Russell has me laughing. He's telling some stupid story about people at his work, and I can't help myself. Mom made scalloped potatoes and steak, and she bought a ridiculously large cake for dessert. I'm heading towards the fridge to get another beer when I hear the front door rattle. The porch light is on and I clearly see a shadow move in front of the frosted glass.

There's a knock at the door.

I can't move; I just watch the shadow, expecting the door to fly open any second now.

Russell appears. He stares at me with a look of confusion that quickly fades into one of concern. I expect him to tell me I'm being silly but all he does is nod. He goes to front door and I'm holding my breath. He opens it.

Jay, Kevin's brother, stands in the doorway. He's wearing jeans, a bulky winter jacket and a tuque. He's got a clean and empty casserole dish in his hands. As soon as I see it's him, my fear and anxiety fade, but they're quickly replaced by something else. Guilt.

"My mom wanted me to give this back to Mrs. Dufault," Jay says. Even though I'm right behind Russell, he's doing a good job of not looking at me.

"Jay, is that you?" My mother's voice comes from the living room. "Why don't you come in for a second? We're just having dessert."

Jay grimaces and his eyes flick to me. "No thanks, Mrs. Dufault." He clears his throat and passes the dish to Russell. "I need to get back to my mom. Things to do, you know?"

My mom leaves the table and comes to stand beside Russell, nearly blocking my view of the door. "Are you sure?"

He nods and bites his lip. "I was wondering, though . . . Could I speak to Clive for a second? Alone?"

I'm not sure I want to talk to Jay. I've never liked him, but I feel I owe him something. I have no idea why I feel guilty. Rationally, I know I'm not to blame for Kevin's death. But my inner critic wonders if he'd still be alive if I didn't drink as much that night. If Kevin had gone home instead of crashing at my place, would he have been taken?

"It's okay, Mom," I say. Slipping on my shoes and coat, I walk past them out onto the front porch. She gives me this look like I'm a delicate flower that's going to crack or something. Crap. There I go mixing my metaphors again. Russell is frowning at me like he's afraid I'm not strong enough. But he's too nice to ever say something like that. He might think it, but he'd never say it.

Time to man up. I instantly hate myself for sounding like my father. I close the door, and I'm alone out there in the night with Jay.

"How you holding up?" he asks me.

I shrug. "I should be asking you that. The whole thing is . . . unreal, man."

He nods. His eyes are red from crying. "Yeah. You're all over the news, by the way."

"How? Why?"

He looks away. "One of your neighbours took video of you in the lobby. During your. . . moment."

"Please tell me you're joking." I feel sick.

"They've also got you leaving the police station. So, you're famous." He shakes his head. "Anyway, I came back to help with funeral arrangements. Mom's a total disaster. Kevin was always her favorite."

"Ah, don't say that."

He waves my words away. "Nah, it's okay. I know it's true. Kevin was a much better person that I am. I came by earlier today looking for you but when I heard your voice..."

My eyes go wide. "That was you? Shit. You scared the hell out of me."

"Yeah. I figured that. Sorry. It's just . . . as soon as I heard your voice I knew I wasn't ready to talk yet. I need to ask you something and you better fucking tell me the truth.

My brother's all over the news and they're saying . . ." He turns away and holds his head in his hands. "Christ, I know I shouldn't think differently about him, but . . ."

"Kevin's not gay. Those assholes are just trying to sell newspapers or ads or some bullshit. I don't know why that sick bastard chose him or—"

He turns around, his eyes dead still. "Was it you?"

"What?" I told you he was a jerk. "You think that I killed Kevin? You seriously think I'm capable of something like that? Shit."

"Fuck if I know." Jay throws his hands in the air and he looks like he wants to punch me. "Kevin always said you weren't right in the head."

"You fucking piece of shit. He never said that. Never once in his life!"

Jay punches me in the shoulder, but I don't punch back. I just stare at him. He punches me again and jumps off the porch. I wait for him to leave, but he just stands there, the snow crunching beneath his feet. It isn't until he falls to his knees that I see he's crying. I honestly have no clue what I'm supposed to do. I've never liked him, and he just punched me twice after accusing me of being a serial killer. But he's ugly crying in front of me, and Kevin would want me to look after him. I brush the snow off the front porch steps clean with my hand and sit down. I wait, saying nothing. Jay seems to appreciate me being there. A few minutes later he wipes his eyes with the back of his hand and comes to join me on the steps.

"You're right," he says. "Kevin never said you weren't right in the head. Sorry. He said you never really recovered from what that guy Banner did to you."

I hate hearing that name. It's like having my stomach split open.

"Well, I've recovered as much as anyone can," I say. "I think. But no matter how screwed up I am, I would never do anything to hurt your brother. He was like family to me. Back in school, he was the only one who never looked at me differently. Like I was maggot-covered garbage or damaged goods. Fuck. This whole thing is just fucked up. I can't believe he's gone. And not knowing what happened . . ."

I turn to look at Jay but he's staring off into the distance. We stay like that for a few minutes. I can tell he wants to ask me something, but he's not saying the words. I take a guess at what he wants to know.

"The last thing I remember was Kevin taking off my shoes," I say. "I was plastered from all the Jäger bombs, barely conscious. He asked if he could sleep on my couch. That's the last time I saw him."

"So how did he end up in the subway?"

"They found his body?"

Jay nods. "Yeah. Last night. It was in an abandoned subway station, one used in making movies. Bay Lower."

"Never heard of it." I purse my lips and look up at the sky. "No freakin' clue how he ended up there. Did you hear about his apartment? It was tossed. Looks like he went home after my place."

"Nope," he says. "That happened earlier in the day. Didn't they tell you?"

The blood drains from my face. "What are you talking about?"

Jay turns to look me in the eye. "My mom talked to some detective today. He said they were able to fix the time of the break-in at my brother's place to when we were at the bar. Also, the blood on the floor wasn't his."

"Are you shittin' me?" I lean back, shaking my head. "Someone broke into his apartment while we were out drinking? Says who?"

Jay shrugs. "Something about a noise complaint or something. They didn't go into details. All I know is that while we were out, someone tossed his apartment. The next day he ends up dead. Ask me, I don't think this has anything to do with the gay serial killer. Maybe someone just wanted it to look like it's related to throw us off."

I'm starting to think the same thing, but it sounds farfetched. "Still doesn't make any sense. Kevin didn't have enemies. It was impossible to hate him."

"I know," Jay says. "I tried to hate him, but I couldn't."

We sit silently for a few more minutes and slowly an uncomfortable thought solidifies for me. "So, he never went home. Kevin really was taken from my apartment."

Jay stands up. "Looks like. But there was no sign of a struggle at your place, was there? And from what I've heard, there's no video of Kevin leaving through the front door. That's why I asked if it was you. People that go through things like you did . . . sometimes they aren't right in the head after. Even if my brother would never say that. But . . . I never really believed you killed him. I heard how you reacted when they found his body. Damn. So weird saying that. His body." He puts his hands on his hips and takes a few deep breaths. "Look, I know everyone thinks I'm a jerk. Maybe I am. But Kev was my brother. I need to know what happened."

I think about saying something as he walks away but keep quiet.

Everyone assumes things get better with closure. They're wrong. The incident from when I was twelve . . . I have as much closure as you could ask for. The guy went to jail. The maximum amount you can get for sexual assault on a minor is only fourteen years. But because of what he did to the others, he's away for multiple murders. I won't have to worry about him being on the streets for a good long time. Still doesn't help much.

I look at my hands. At the pale scars from where he put the nail gun. Thunk thunk. I can still hear the sound of each nail as he . . .

I push the thoughts away. Dwelling on it never does me any good. Especially if I'm standing outside in the dark. Alone.

When I walk back inside, I find my mom and Russell sitting on the sofa, their eyes glued to the TV. They haven't turned on the living room lights, so their faces are illuminated by this strange blue glow, and it looks kind of beautiful. Peaceful. I notice my mom is biting her nails, and Russell looks like he wants to throw up.

"What's wrong?" I ask. "Is it more about Kevin?"

My mom shakes her head. "You don't need to watch this, dear."

"Come on, Alison," Russell says. "You can't shelter him from this. He's going to find out." He exhales slowly and mutes the TV. "It's not Kevin. They found another body. A woman."

CHAPTER TWELVE

"Whaaat?" I sit on the sofa next to my mom trying to catch up on the news. I see video of a crime scene. A black body bag on an ambulance gurney, flashing police lights and crowds. "And they think it's the same killer? I thought he only killed guys?"

My mom puts her hand on my knee. "Are you sure you have to go back to Toronto? I'm not certain it's a safe place for you to be anymore. What with the killing and . . ."

"Mom. I'm not a child. Thanks, but . . ." Deep breath. "If it's a woman, why do they think it's the same killer?"

Russell presses a button on the remote and the TV starts rewinding. Nice feature being able to rewind "live TV". Yay, technology.

I recognize the reporter from the local Toronto station. "Disturbing news tonight suggests no one is safe from the Plastic Strangler." Yep. That's seriously what they're calling him. Lame. "The latest victim is twenty-four-year-old Monica Bailey, a . . ."

I can tell the reporter is still talking but I can't make out any of the words. Why? Because they flashed a picture of the victim on screen – an attractive redhead with a huge smile. She's leaning up against the white wooden fence along a mountain trail or something. Lots of trees in the background. It takes me all of two seconds to recognize her.

"That's her," I say. "That's the woman from the video."

My mom looks over at me. "You know her?"

Russell turns in his seat to look at me. "Which video are you talking about, Son?"

I wince. I hate when he calls me that. "Do you have that detective's number? Mr. Coyle. I need to call him. Right now."

My fight/flight response, telling me that I should stay out of this. In the movies, anytime an amateur detective starts investigating a string of murders, they always end up dead. Or at least being chased by the killer. But that doesn't count for me, does it? I'm already mixed up in this thing. I just don't know how.

***

Mom stands in the doorway of the computer room, not letting me close the door. "What's going on, Clive? Why do you need the computer?"

I push her back a bit. "I told you, I talked with Detective Coyle on the phone and he needs me to email him a link."

"But why do you need the door closed?"

I blush and try to stay calm. "Good night, Mom. It's late. I'll see you in the morning. Love you."

She opens her mouth, and I can tell she wants to say something else. I close the door before she gets a chance.

It takes me forever to connect with Coyle. Not surprising, really, considering the new murder. When I tell him, I recognized the latest victim, Monica Bailey, from the sex tape in my office building, he asks me to send him the link to the video. He says it's faster doing that than having his staff dig through the thousands of videos on the site.

I sit down at my mom's computer and see that the curtains are open. Even though there aren't any houses behind ours, I shut the curtains. Looking at porn in my mom's place makes me super uncomfortable. But I'm not really looking at porn, am I? I'm helping the police with an investigation.

I log into the tube site with my username and password and search through my favorites for the video. Yes, I added it to my favorites. Don't judge me. It was super hot. Although, as soon as I see the thumbnail for the video, I feel an ickiness in my gut. Seeing Monica naked, her head thrown back and her arms behind her . . . I don't know. It feels kind of like a violation now. It was different when she wasn't a real person, when I didn't know her name. And now she's dead and the other guy in the video is probably Jerry Tran, also dead. It doesn't seem so hot anymore.

I open my Gmail account in a second tab, copy the URL into a message and email it off to Coyle. I also include the username of the weird comment: Matt Elliott. I'm sure it's a waste of time. No one uses their real name on those sites. Although maybe if the sicko is really far gone he might. Anyway, cops in the movies always have ways of tracking down people on the internet. Worth a chance anyway.

After I send the email, logic brain tells me to turn off the computer and go to bed. Inner critic has other ideas. It needs to understand what is happening or it won't shut down. It whispers: What percent of all murders are ever solved? Damn. I know the way my mind works. Disturbing question or not, there's no way I'll get any sleep tonight until I have an answer.

I end up on the Stats Canada webpage where they proudly proclaim that most murders in Canada are solved. I see the number – seventy-six percent.

"Christ. That's horrible. That means almost a third of all murders go unsolved." I look up how many people were murdered last year. A quick search shows me Canada had just over six hundred murders last year. I Google the number for the United States for comparison – almost fifteen thousand. To be fair, Canada has a much smaller population, around thirty-five million Canadians compared to three-hundred and sixteen million Americans. Still, thirty-three percent of either amount is a disturbing number. Last year, in Canada alone, two hundred people were murdered, and their killers were never caught. My locked doors make me feel even less safe now.

I go back to the tube site. Even though Monica's video is spoiled for me now there are all these naked women in front of me. I feel the urge to masturbate. My mother coughs in the next room, and the urge goes away.

I stare at the login name: Matt Elliott. "What the heck. Let's Google it."

Not surprisingly, this doesn't help at all. There's dozens of Matt Elliotts from around the world. And it's most likely not even the commenter's real name anyway. My username is Ethan Strider, which is actually a play on words. You see, I'm beyond obsessed with an old TV show called Veronica Mars. One of the main characters on that show was played by the amazing Jason Dohring, who is a close runner-up to Chris Pratt for my ideal man crush. Anyway, Jason Dohring later appeared on another of my favorite shows, Supernatural, as a character named Ethan Snyder, a time-traveling immortal. Time-travelling immortals, like Dr. Who, are cool. Also, Ethan Strider would make a perfect porn star name.

Gears in my head start spinning. If I took that much time to think about my username, maybe this Matt Elliott did as well. Maybe, just maybe, his username means something after all.

Usernames on the tube site are all hyperlinks. I click on it and go to Matt Elliott's profile page. Hardly any of the details are filled out, but I see his fake profile picture, the one of a topless Ryan Gosling. He's been a member for three years. There's a button for me to subscribe to his feed so I can automatically see any videos he posts or likes. I've never really understood why anyone would want to subscribe to what someone else whacks off to, but to each his own.

There's actually room for tons of stats – age, eye color, number of friends, heck even what sign he is. He has almost four thousand fans. For a weird minute I'm super jealous because he has way more fans than I do. The only info he's filled out aside from his username is his location, Toronto, and gender, male.

Beneath his profile picture is a log of his activity, the videos he likes and comments on. It's kind of like the Facebook of porn. There's even a button saying, "Click here to chat with Matt Elliott." I think about doing that for all of two seconds before I realize how immensely stupid that would be.

I scroll through videos he's commented on. Then I see it – a thumbnail of Monica standing on a beach, fully clothed and smiling. The video is called "Sunnyside Seduction" so I assume it's from the local waterfront park of the same name. I glance at the door, make sure the volume is muted, and click play.

The video starts with someone videotaping the waves. Kids build sandcastles close to the shore. Joggers run by alone or in pairs. It narrows in on a one woman walking by herself. Monica. She's wearing blue walking shorts and a crimson blouse. As she approaches the camera, Monica stops. She says something to the person taping. A moment later she is smiling and looking around. The video skips, and I see a masculine hand pass Monica a hundred-dollar bill. She looks around again before putting the money in her purse. She undoes the buttons on her blouse, revealing the cream-colored bra beneath.

The video skips ahead a bit further. There is another exchange of money and Monica points toward the back of a nearby building. The camera follows her. Occasionally, Monica says something and looks around shyly.

She walks around the building and stands beside a parked SUV. She's smiling again, a seductive look on her face as she completely removes her top. She plays with her left nipple and sticks her tongue out at the camera. She stops, listening for a moment, spins, arms over her head.

Monica's face changes. She looks angry, insulted. She puts her shirt back on and starts to walk away. Whoever is filming her follows. She waves him away, but something makes her stop. She turns, frowns, and holds out her hand. Three more hundreds are exchanged.

"This is weird," I mumble, but can't stop watching.

Monica looks around, shrugs, and undoes the buttons on her shorts. She slides them down to her knees, revealing her underwear. They aren't overly flattering but I've learned that women usually don't dress like Victoria's Secret models. Men have been lied to. Although, honestly, it was probably men lying to ourselves. She pushes her underwear down, showing her shaved pubic area. The camera zooms in.

"Damn it. I need to hear this. Need my headphones."

Paranoia drives me to close the browser and clear the cache. Although it's doubtful my mom or Russell will come in to check what I've been doing, I'd rather not take chances and avoid an uncomfortable conversation. I go back to my room, dig through my backpack for my sleep headphones, and go back to the computer room. It takes me a few seconds to find the slot for headphones on Mom's new speakers. Once they're firmly in place I bring up the video again, fast forward to the part where I left off, and press play.

"Good enough?" Monica asks. Again it hits me how macabre this is, watching videos of a recently-dead person doing naked sexy stuff. Her voice is deep and throaty, playful.

"Yes." The second voice is male, probably the same person holding the camera. It doesn't sound like a serial killer's voice. Instead, the man's voice is light, almost musical. He has a slight accent but I can't place it. "That's beautiful. Are you interested in earning even more money?"

Monica laughs and shakes her head. "Nah. I think that's as far as this girl needs to go. Thanks for the money, though. It's been fun."

The camera zooms in on her face. "Please reconsider. You're beautiful."

"Momma warned me about guys like you." Monica pulls her shorts up and rebuttons them. "I've never done anything like this before. Thank you for the experience."

"It's bad luck not to finish what you start."

Monica winks at the camera. "I'll take my chances."

The man says nothing. The camera pulls back, focused only on Monica as she walks away. She only looks over her shoulder once. As she leaves, the man starts whispering something, but I can't make it out. I rewind the video and turn up the volume. Now the voice is clearer. Audible.

"Stupid cow," the man says. "Don't say I didn't warn you. Now you're on the list."

I stop the video, totally creeped out. That's pretty much what he said in the comment on the bathroom video, the one with maybe-Jerry-Tran. I wondered if Monica even knew about this video. What if it was done with a hidden camera? Maybe Jerry Tran was killed because he knew Monica. I'm about to send Coyle another email providing the link to this video when I see another familiar face.

Kevin.

"No fucking way." The thumbnail shows Kevin sitting on a park bench. The title is "Abercrombie Behind the Bush." I'm completely torn. I know I have to watch the video. This is the first clear link between Kevin and another victim. I wonder how far Kevin went, but I'm also afraid to find out.

I click play. The man with the light voice starts talking.

"Here we are in Toronto looking for a new actor. Lots of pretty faces around. Let's see how lucky we are today."

He goes up to woman dressed in a jogging suit. He interrupts her mid-stretch as she prepares for a run. He asks her a few questions. It's immediately obvious she has no time to play these games. She runs away. He approaches a man with brown hair and a beard. This one won't even stop to speak to him for a minute. The scene chances and the camera focuses on Kevin eating his lunch in the park on a bright sunny day. The date stamp on the video says it was uploaded in August. I recognize the location – Victoria Memorial Square.

"Got a minute there, buddy?" says the guy behind the camera. The more I hear the guy talk, the more I notice a slight accent. Perhaps East Coast. The only person I've ever heard say "buddy" like that was my friend Scott Stevens from Dartmouth, Nova Scotia.

Kevin looks annoyed. "Not really. I only have a few minutes for lunch." He's wearing a white dress shirt, black slacks and a red tie. He told me he hated having to dress like this for work. He was always more comfortable in jeans.

"Sorry, I won't take up much of your time. I'm just—"

"What's with the video camera? Dude, turn that shit off." Well, that answers that. The camera was visible. So Monica knew she was making a video.

Camera Guy laughs. "Sorry. It's for a school project. I'm doing a survey on the types of jobs people will do when they need more money. Have you ever thought of getting a second job to help pay the bills?"

Kevin sighs and takes a bite of his sandwich. "Sure. Everyone does."

"What if there was a way for you to earn an extra hundred dollars? Would you be interested?"

"Depends what I have to do." Kevin is staring at the camera now like he wants to punch something. "Where's this going?"

"Like I said, just a school project. Have you ever considered being a male model before?"

Kevin laughs and looks away. "Get real. Although one of my friends says I look like an Abercrombie and Fitch model. If you can believe that."

Crap. He's talking about me.

"Oh, I can believe it. Can I ask you a few quick questions?"

"Sure," Kevin says. He finishes his sandwich, checks his watch and wipes his hands off on his pants. "You have ten minutes. Shoot."

"We'll start with an easy one. How old are you?"

"Twenty-one. Why?"

"Just establishing a demographic. Are you married or single? Any girlfriend or boyfriend?"

"Single. No girlfriend."

"So you prefer women?"

Kevin glances at his watch again. "Look, if you're trying to come on to me or—"

"Nothing like that. Nothing like that. Simple questions. What type of women do you like?"

"Older women. Early thirties." Kevin looks a bit devilish now. Probably thinking about one of the MILFs he's done recently.

"Have you ever had sex in a public place?"

Kevin laughs. "Sure."

Looking down I see the video is over twenty minutes long. I skip ahead a bit. Video guy hands Kevin a hundred dollars. Kevin holds it up as if checking to see if it's real or counterfeit. He pockets it and pulls his shirttails out. He's lifting his shirt to show his abs. Video guy laughs.

"Very good. Very good. You must work out."

Kevin lifts the shirt a little higher so the camera can fully capture his six-pack. He lets the shirt fall back and looks at his watch again. He starts to stand when video guy passes him two more hundred-dollar bills. Kevin looks at the money but doesn't stop tucking in his shirt again.

Video guy adds another hundred to the pile. "Are you interested in earning a little more money?"

Kevin shakes his head. "Lunch is over."

"Nothing difficult. I promise. I'd really like the see the rest of your body."

"Sorry, dude. Not gay. Best of luck, though."

"Ah, come." Video guy adds two more hundred-dollar bills. "Isn't it worth being late to work for all this money? Unless you make five hundred dollars an hour."

Kevin stops and looks around. "Nope. Not that much. But it's a career. If anyone at work ever sees this video I'm_"

"Don't worry. I told you this is only for a—"

"Yeah, yeah, yeah. And give me one good reason why I'd believe anything you say. I don't know you, dude. This is as far as I go."

Kevin is walking away. Video guy is mumbling to himself again.

"So that's it." I take off my headphones and step away from the computer. I pace back and forth in the computer room and feel a strong need for beer. "This guy propositions people to make sex tapes. If they turn him down, he . . . kills them? That seems a tad extreme." I copy the URL for Kevin's video and paste it in the email I'm going to send Coyle when I notice another video by the same user.

It's one of the creepiest things I've ever seen.

I mean like Rob-Zombie creepy.

A man, naked, standing in a bathtub. He's extremely skinny like me with nearly-white blond hair. His entire body is covered with red welts. I've watched enough porn to know what these are – whip marks. Behind him, dozens of hard plastic figures representing shapely men and women, naked: Lillie and Jack dolls. The man's hands are out in front of him, hiding his crotch. His fingernails are painted black and he's wearing silver rings on every finger. He looks familiar, but it takes me a few minutes to place him.

"Holy shit," I say. "That's Michael. The first victim."

I press play and hear the same voice again. Video guy. He's giving instructions to Michael, telling him where to touch his own body, how to stand. Michael appears to be enjoying it. He has an erection, and he keeps blowing kisses towards the camera. The two men banter back and forth with each other. I'm no detective but it sounds like they know each other. Maybe they're friends. Maybe they're dating.

I'm going to say something now, and at first you're going to think this is weird. But stay with me. I don't really understand why people make sex tapes. Not the types of tapes I've made. That I get. What I mean is, why would people in a loving, committed relationship take videos of themselves in foreplay or sex? Anyone with half a brain knows there's a market for that sort of thing. All it takes is an angry ex, and your private video isn't so private anymore. Unless that's the point. Maybe people make sex tapes because they want people to see them. They need to have people see them just like I do.

Michael leans over, puts his right index finger up his ass and starts licking the featureless crotches of the dolls on the wall. A fist punches out, hitting Michael in the gut, but it's not a normal fist. It's covered in some sort of black latex like a catsuit. Michael grunts, then coos, pleading for more. Someone steps out in front of the camera – a woman with a platinum blond wig wearing a dominatrix outfit. The woman turns to face the camera, and I see it's not really a woman at all. The plastic face is crude and unnaturally smooth. Fake blue eyes and bright scarlet lips are painted on the face. She looks like a mockery of a Lillie doll, complete with gigantic bubble breasts. A real-life sex doll.

"Someone's been naughty," video guy says. It seems like the voice is coming from behind the mask, but it's hard to tell. The lips don't move. There are small openings in each iris and I can see eyes peaking out through them. "He needs to be punished."

The creepy, living sex doll picks something up from the floor. It's a long, thing metal spike. She grabs Michael's penis with one hand and . . .

"I'm out!" I throw the headphones off and avert my eyes, trying not to see what's happening on the screen as I press stop.

You hear people talk about triggers, things that set off bad memories in rape victims. It's all over the media now, but unless you've experienced it you have no idea what it's like. I was perfectly okay up until the spike. It became something else completely. Just that one thing, and I'm back in the basement, like I'm living through it all over again.

I stare at my hands, at the small scar on each palm. I've never been able to touch a nail. Not since that day.

As soon as my hands stop shaking, I send a second email to Coyle with the URLs of the other videos.

After I send the email with the multiple video links to Coyle, I clear the cache again and delete the browsing history. I install and run a program called CCleaner, because I know searching online leaves tons of traces. My mom would freak out enough to know I'm looking at porn. If she sees I'm looking at gay porn . . . Well, let's just say that's a conversation I'd rather not have. Ever.

As I head back to my bedroom, my inner critic starts whispering doubts. Maybe Video Guy isn't the killer. It could all be a coincidence, right?

"I don't believe in coincidence," I say to no one. When things look connected it probably means there is a connection. Maybe if I looked just a little bit longer, I could find it. But I know how my obsessive behavior works. I need to let this go or it will consume me. "I've done my part. More than my part. The police have a few leads to follow up on now. The rest is up to them."

CHAPTER THIRTEEN

I sleep maybe a few hours that night, even with the help of several beers, valerian root, and my binaural beats. I can't get those videos out of my head. And I feel guilty about watching the one with Kevin. I'm super relieved he didn't do anything too extreme. That is not how I want to remember my friend.

I stumble out of bed around seven, in time to eat breakfast with my mom and Russell. Mom asks how long I'm going to stay but. I haven't given it much thought. I also realize it's Friday. I completely forgot to call in to work and let them know I wasn't coming in yesterday or today.

Crap. I quickly explain and ask if I can make a long-distance call. Mom looks to Russell, which is kind of weird. Like why does she need his permission to let her son make a phone call? But whatever. They let me make it. I call in and leave a message for my manager, who obviously won't be in at that time in the morning. I tell her my friend was killed last night and I need time off work. I tell her my phone's broken and leave my mom's number as a contact.

Mom puts a spare key on the counter before she leaves. She says I should get out, grab some fresh air. The snow has stopped and the sun's shining. I say I'll consider it.

A few hours later, my manager calls back and tells me everything's cool. She saw me on the news and didn't expect me to come in. She tells me I can take next week off work if I need it. She's already cleared it with HR. They'll count it as sick time, so I won't even have to use up vacation. I'm so grateful I'm on the verge of gushing. The last thing I need is getting fired in the middle of all this.

I have the next week off work, an entire week with nothing to do. Immediately, I regret it. I need something to take my mind off this. Kevin's death, the serial killer, Michael in the bathtub.

"I'm never going to un-see that," I mumble. I go to the fridge and grab a beer. I glance at the clock on the wall. Its not even ten in the morning, so I put the beer back. Ten minutes later I'm reaching into the fridge again because fuck it, that's why.

I take the beer to the living room and turn on the TV. I watch an old X-Men cartoon. Cyclops is my favorite. No matter what life throws at him, he just takes charge and handles it. Although, let's be honest. I would totally do Rogue. And Storm. Maybe Rogue and Storm at the same time. And it's right about then I know I need to masturbate.

I put my hand down my pants, but I can still smell my mom's perfume in the air. Eddy is on the couch opposite me, blinking slowly at me, like he's wondering what the fuck I'm doing. I pull out my hand and look around.

"This is stupid," I say. "Why can't I jerk off here?" I was a teenager in this house. Trust me, it's been done before. But I'm an adult now. Somehow, it just feels different. Disrespectful and icky. This little part of my brain keeps saying it's not beyond the realm of possibility that Mom or Russell could come home early. I love the thrill of being in public, the risk of being caught, but not by them. Gross.

I go to the bathroom, lock the door and start stroking myself, but it's not happening. Which makes me even more desperate to get off. So I throw on some clothes, grab the spare key, and call a cab.

I head to Lynden Park Mall. It's pretty pathetic as far as malls go, but it's the best one in Brantford. Jerking off in public is probably not what Mom was thinking when she said I should get some air, but this will get my head straight much more than a walk will.

I start at Bath & Body Works. I stand in the candle section, stroking myself with one hand as I pretend to look at three varieties of vanilla-scented tea lights. Nearby, a group of women are talking with a sales associate about different types of peppermint hand lotion. They're no more than ten feet away. I brush my hands against my nipples and already I'm feeling better.

I grab a coffee at Timmies and I go sit in the food court. I sip my double double and unzip my pants. A security guy is looking at me strangely, so I wink at him. He shakes his head and wanders away. I made sure not to wear underwear so I'd have easier access. I reach in and pull my junk out. I sit like that for about fifteen minutes. I flip it back in, zip up my pants and head to the bathroom.

As soon as I'm in the stall my pants are around my ankles and I'm stroking myself. I hear the sound of people coming and going. Toilets flush. People cough. I leave the stall unlocked and peak out the gap between door and wall. I take off my coat and hang it on the back of the door. I take off my shirt. I'm basically naked surrounded by all these people and I am so hard.

It takes ten minutes but finally there are no sounds at all.

I open the stall door and take a step forward. I stand there, completely exposed, looking at myself in the mirror over the sinks. Any second now and someone could walk in and . . .

I explode. I make sure to lean forward so that I shoot on the floor and don't get any on me. The next time someone comes in, it will be the first thing they see. Which means I need to haul ass and get out of there.

Quickly, I get back into the stall and close the door. My heart is pounding as I get dressed. I feel completely high, a million times better. My mind is crystal clear.

I'm doing up my pants when I hear footsteps approach. Panic like you wouldn't believe takes me over.

I hold my breath. Sure, they won't catch me red-handed, but this is pretty fucking close. My cum is on the floor outside only a few feet from me. It won't take much to see what I've done, to call the cops. My mom will find out, and it's all downhill from there.

I hear someone pissing at the urinal. I open the stall door a crack and peek out. It's some young punk with dyed black hair and big headphones on. He's flipping through his phone as he takes a leak, completely oblivious to everything else.

I push the door open all the way and get my ass out of there. I count myself lucky he was so distracted he didn't see the cum on the tiles. I remind myself to stay calm as I leave the bathroom and walk out of the mall. If I start running, security will zone in on me. If I can just manage to look normal, no one will notice me.

As soon as I'm outside, this enormous depression crashes into me and I start crying. At first I don't know why I'm sad. Then it hits me. No one saw me. Maybe no one ever really sees me, and that's the problem, isn't it? Maybe if I felt really seen I wouldn't do this. Or maybe this is me trying to assign rational reasons for irrational behavior. Honestly, I don't have a fucking clue why I do what I do.

It's snowing again. Soft, wet flakes swirl around in a way that is comforting, rather than hostile. Some snow makes you want to hide indoors. This makes me want to explore. And suddenly I know where I have to go.

Back to the old house.

I use a payphone – because, believe it or not, Brantford is stuck in a time warp and actually still has pay phones – and call a cab. There's no way he'll take me where I really want to go, so I pick the next closest place.

"Lion's Park Arena," I say. That gets me a weird look, mostly because it's way too early in the day for a game, but it's better than revealing my actual destination. The arena is clear on the other side of Brantford, which in a way is nice, like I'm getting a small tour of my hometown. I've only been gone a few years but already there are some big changes. They cleaned up downtown so it doesn't look like the set of a horror film anymore. Here's a fun fact. You know that movie Silent Hill? Yeah, that was filmed in downtown Brantford. If you'd seen it back when I was young, well, let's just say they didn't have to add much in the way of special effects to make the place look creepy.

The cabbie drops me off outside the arena. I wait until he leaves, then head away from the arena and towards the river. Towards the forest.

Course, it's not a real forest, but I grew up in the city. I thought anything with more than five trees constituted a forest. And this section of river front has significantly more than five. The Grand River is more than two hundred and seventy kilometers long. Its banks are spotted with large sections of green space – tall trees and hiking trails. This particular section used to be my playground. Up until the incident, I lived in the Chiefswood Trailer Park on the other side of the Grand. Parents always told us kids to stay away from the woods. Of course we completely didn't listen. I played hide and seek in those trees with Kevin and Jay. Sometimes I'd go there alone and wander. It felt magical, like if I took the right path at the right time, I could leave this world behind and end up in another place – a magical world filled with dragons and adventure.

And then, one day in the woods, I met a monster.

The closer I get to the trees, the more I question my sanity. I mean, seriously, of all the places I could go, why they hell was I coming here? Recent events have brought everything back to the surface. It's not my first time back, but I haven't been here in years. I know I'm being stupid.

There are no answers beneath the dead snow-covered branches. But I keep going anyway.

All the trails are covered in snow, and I'm wearing the worst possible shoes for this. A few seconds in, snow slips over the upper edges of my running shoes. It melts as soon as it hits the heat of my socked feet. So now I'm cold and my feet are wet. A normal person would turn around and get out of there. I keep going.

The world grows quiet. The sounds of the city fade the farther into the woods I go. I smile, remembering how magical it felt here as a child.

Something cracks nearby.

I jump, spinning to look for the source. I see nothing and take a deep breath.

"Chill, Clive," I mumble. "Probably just a squirrel in the underbrush. Or something."

Farther in, the snow stops falling. I actually feel warmer, probably because the trees are blocking the cold wind. I see the old house. I stare at peeling paint and boarded-up windows, not really sure what to feel. Years ago, this house functioned as a tourist center. Now, it looks like the house from Texas Chainsaw Massacre. The tourist centre was only open in the summer. Banner took us in the winter. No one even thought to look here, not at first.

I walk up to the front door and pull on the handle. Of course it's locked. All the windows are boarded up. The sick part of my brain that brought me here actually wants to go inside. I turn and put my back to the door, lean back and look out over the woods. Everything is covered with a pristine layer of white.

"Beautiful." I smile and try to figure out what I'm feeling. Should I feel something being here again, back where it happened? You'd think I'd feel terrified, but it wasn't the place that hurt me. It was a man. And that man is still in my head. My mind is far more terrifying than this forest.

"Caw!"

I jump, nearly slipping on the snow-covered steps, and look above me. Two black crows are perched on the roof.

"Shit." I exhale slowly and scratch my head. "I'll take that as my cue to get out of here."

The crows caw in unison again and memories flood through me, so strong that it's not like a memory at all. More like I'm living through it all over again.

***

I open my eyes and don't know where I am. Soft bluish light seeps in through a small nearby window. I see wooden beams above me and cobwebs. I turn to the window and my sight lands on my arm. I feel groggy like I'm on cold medication. My brain isn't working right. I take in the rest of my body. I'm only wearing underwear.

A centipede crawls up my bare leg. I try to bat it away, but my hands won't move. Only then do I feel my hands are restrained. Not by rope, but by some sort of plastic tie. And it all comes crashing in on me. Even at that age, I'd seen enough TV to know what was happening to me.

I get so scared I piss myself. I pull at the restraints but they're too strong. I try screaming but my mouth won't open. I try to think of ways to escape but my head is too foggy. I know I must have been drugged, and now I'm even more scared. I can't imagine being any more terrified.

That's when I see the others.

There are four of us, all boys I know from the trailer park. Each of us is tied to a support beam, each of us stripped down to our undergarments. One boy is covered in blood. He's not moving. The others are all looking at me, eyes wide, shaking their heads violently. One, Todd Michaluk, has a big black bruise on his chest. He's older than me, maybe thirteen, I think. And that's when it hits me – Todd went missing last week. The police went door to door asking if anyone had seen him. People said he'd run away. His dad was a total dick, so it was believable.

But if Todd has been here for a week and no one has found him, that means no one will find me either.

I cry and pull at my restraints. The plastic restraints cut into my wrists. It's so painful but I keep struggling.

Above me, the floorboards creak. The other boys go statue-still. It's so quiet it feels like everyone is holding their breath. A door opens. Heavy footsteps walk down wooden stairs off to the right. I look over and see the monster again. Banner.

I know I've been drugged. My brain feels foggy, disconnected, and something looks off about Banner, like he's not alone. The shadows behind him seem to swirl for a moment, a trick of the light amplified by whatever he's given me to keep me calm. I know it's impossible, but for just a moment it feels like the shadows are watching me.

Banner unzips a thick winter coat. He's wearing a red plaid shirt beneath, which, with his thick, black beard, makes him look like a real lumberjack. He looks over his shoulder like he's listening to the shadows. I see his lips move. He's talking to someone who isn't there. He walks over to a nearby bench and picks up something.

A nail gun.

***

One of the crows caws again, and I walk away from the house. I focus on the sound of the snow crunching beneath my feet to block out the memory of the nail gun. And what Banner did to Todd.

Once I'm back at the arena, I call another cab and head home. I'm back before Mom and Russell and grab another beer. I swallow four valerian root pills and lie down. I want to sleep, to make it all go away, but my mind is still back in the basement. I need something to distract me.

With a sigh, I go do the one thing I've been putting off for days. I check Facebook. The last time I logged in I saw Kevin's body. For once it's not all stupid cat videos, updates from celebrities on films they're shooting or fancy restaurants they've eaten at. Instead, everyone is posting pictures of themselves with Kevin, talking about how amazing he was. People I have a vague connection with tell me how sorry they are for my loss. Pretty soon I'm a complete basket case, crying quietly as I scroll through the images. I respond to some of the private messages, only the ones from good friends and family I'm close with.

I notice a private message from Delilah and I sit up a little straighter. Seeing her name and her picture makes me smile. So does her message.

"You must be devastated. Let me be there for you. Here's my number. I hope you call but I completely understand if you need time alone. I'll keep you in my thoughts, beautiful."

Honest to god, I actually blush. She called me beautiful. I know guys aren't supposed to be beautiful. We're strong, handsome, but not beautiful. Somehow, having her call me that makes me feel like everything could be okay with the world. Not now, of course, but someday.

I realize I totally miss her. I want her to be with me here, right now. I want to call her, to hear her voice, but she's still at work. I could call her at work, but I know my mom would question the long-distance phone call. Seriously, not having a phone sucks. So instead, I message Delilah back on Facebook.

I let her know I'm staying with my mom, and before I can think myself out of doing it, I tell her I miss her. After I click send I wait for a response. Ten minutes later there's still no response.

I smack my head. "Of course there's no response, idiot. She's at work. This isn't a text message and they don't exactly let us surf Facebook at our desks."

I log out of Facebook and check my email, looking to see if Coyle has responded to my emails. Nothing. So I spend the next hour or so reading every news story I can find about the killings in Toronto.

I try to imagine what Veronica Mars would do. She'd create a murder board with pictures of the victims and crime scene photos. Veronica would pin a map to the wall marking out the locations where the bodies were found. She'd follow the money, find out what each person did for a living and somehow get access to all their banking and credit card info. Okay, so I don't have magical detective powers, but I do have Facebook and Google maps.

I already learned they found victim number one, Michael Needs, at his dorm room. Five more minutes of searching confirms he lived at Pittman Hall Residence, close to Ryerson University. I can't find any evidence he had a job.

Victim number two, Fred Dimmerman, was from Scarborough and worked in a comic book store on Yonge St. A bit more digging and I realize his body was actually found in a house on Runnymede, way over in the West Bloor Village.

The third victim, Ethan Marchese, a bartender at a bar called Woodies, was found in his apartment at 730 Ontario Street. By this point, I realize the murderer is not trying to draw a pentagram over the city, so I can rule out demonic conjurations.

But I am seeing a pattern.

The first three bodies were all found within a few city blocks of a subway station. Which I realize might not be a pattern at all. Driving in Toronto sucks ass, but the transit system isn't bad. There are stations everywhere.

I can't find any info online about where Kevin's body was found, which probably means the police are keeping it quiet. The most they say is his body was found in an "unused" section of subway. Jay called it Bay Lower. I do a quick Google search on unused sections of the Toronto Subway. Surprisingly, I find out there two. Trains still pass through Bay Lower, but it's been closed to the general public since 1966. Another, called Queen Lower, looks completely abandoned and doesn't even have live tracks. If Kevin's body had been placed there, it wouldn't have been found so quickly.

Monica Bailey, twenty-four, was an investment banker. She was found at 15 Windermere Avenue, a significantly more up-scale area than the others. It's a high-rise condo that looks out over the lake. Google Maps shows me it's also not far from Sunnyside Park, where Monica's video was shot.

"Huh." I push back from the computer and shake my head. "It doesn't fit the pattern. That place is nowhere near a subway line."

It hits me.

I've forgotten a murder. Jerry Tran. I already know that's near the subway. And there's Kevin's boss. What happened to him? I don't have much to go on, not even his name. He could be alive and well in another office.

Aside from the nameless boss, only Monica's death doesn't fit the pattern. If what I'm seeing is actually a pattern at all. I mean, Pittman Hall isn't really that close to a subway station. Like it's close if you look at a map, but not if you have to walk the streets.

I pull a few more rabbits out of my crime-solving, TV show hat. I Google all the names of the victims, checking to see if I come up with anything significant. Like maybe they are all characters in a movie or some obscure book. Nothing. I look up the dates of the murders and check for significance. If there's a pattern there, I don't see it. I try anagrams, compare the ages of the victims. Nothing. I troll their Facebook pages. All of them, except Monica's, are open to the public, just like their Twitter and Instagram accounts.

I flip through hundreds of pictures of the victims. The more I look, the more convinced I become that I'm missing something.

I can't tell what it is yet, but some piece of this puzzle is off. I know once it comes to me it will be obvious, but for now my mind can't sort it out.

What am I missing?

CHAPTER FOURTEEN

"You don't have to go." Mom has her car keys in one hand, a cup of Timmie's coffee in the other. She's not taking this well. Understandably, she's worried about me. "Kevin's funeral is in a few days, and you said you have the whole week off."

I know she's only trying to be helpful, but this is the fourth time we've had this conversation. It's Saturday morning, and I've asked her to drive me home. I don't respond this time and keep packing. Honestly, I don't want to tell her I'm heading back because I want to see Delilah. If I mention there is a girl involved, my mother will start planning our wedding. She's just like that.

"But it's not safe, Clive." She looks into the kitchen, where Russell is silently eating his breakfast. I notice he's doing a damn fine job of looking like he can't hear us. Mom doesn't look thrilled with him. "I spoke with Russell last night. We both agreed you could stay here for a while, just until–"

"Thanks, Mom." I kiss her on the cheek. "It means a lot to me that you'd be willing to let me move back home. But I am an adult now. I can take care of myself."

Even as I'm saying it, I realize I sure don't I feel like an adult. Part of me does want to just stay here, forget all about Toronto and the life I've built there. I'm scared of going back, but after everything I've seen, I'm pretty convinced I was never the target of the killer. He was after Kevin. If he's attacking people who turned him down for his videos, I'm safe. No one has ever approached me to be in that type of thing.

Sure, a part of me whispers I'm forgetting the whole strange-comment-on-my-video thing, but that's the way my OCD works. These tiny whispers always tell me I'm not doing something I should be doing. Being able to ignore the whispers is the only thing keeping me out of a mental institution.

People have all these misconceptions about obsessive compulsive disorder. That's why I stopped telling people I have it. Usually when I tell someone I have OCD, their eyes light up and they say, "Oh, me too!" And then they talk about all the ways they clean their houses. Christ. Being organized and cleaning up after yourself is not OCD.

So what is it, then? Well, the way Dr. Angus described it to me in therapy is this: the important part isn't the behavior, it's the anxiety that causes the behavior. Human beings have this amazing survival instinct: fight or flight. Whenever we're in a dangerous situation, our bodies change.

We get stronger, faster, smarter, all because we're trying to get away from a threat. Only, in my case, my brain thinks the danger is there all the time. I'm in a near-constant state of fear, only I can't run away, and there's nothing to fight. So instead, these images get stuck in my head and I can't do anything to get rid of them.

No. That's not true. It only feels like I can't do anything to get rid of them. I bury the fear behind routines, little tricks. Doctors label them compulsions, repetitive behavior patterns meant to soften or turn off the intrusive thoughts that get stuck in my head. Some obsess over germs. Not me. I've never been bothered much by the thought of germs. My intrusive thoughts are bigger than that. More focused on reality. I'm terrified that I'm going to be taken again, stolen out of my bedroom while I sleep. Forced to . . .

I push those thoughts away. I have enough control to know the more I allow those fears to settle in me, the worse off I'll be. It's been years since I've had a really bad episode, the type where my mom committed me for my own safety. But that was when I was a minor, back during the trial. I've had it pretty much under control since then.

Like usual, the drive back is long and boring. Mom is a bit tense during the trip, gripping the steering wheel with white-knuckled hands. Maybe it's the freezing rain. The roads are slippery, but people still drive like they're maniacs.

When we get to my apartment, Mom insists on walking me up. I can tell she's being protective, which is sweet and kinda silly. I mean, like, seriously, if there was someone waiting for me in my apartment, what is she going to do about it? Break out her wild mum-fu?

When I walk into the lobby, I head to the security station and identify myself to the guard on duty. This one doesn't look familiar, but I think we've established that doesn't mean a lot. For all I know, he's worked here for years. I show him my ID and he leaves for a second. When he comes back, he has my new set of keys. The landlord did as the police requested and changed the locks. I have to sign some documents before he hands me the keys. This seems to make my mom feel better for some reason.

As expected, my apartment is empty. After a series of hugs and promises to call, I finally get my mom out the door. I lock the door and double check the apartment. I take off the old key from my key ring and put on the new. I sit there on my couch staring at the wall.

I have no idea what I'm supposed to do now.

I flip through the channels on TV, but I'm bored after a few minutes. I play Call of Duty on my PS4 for a few minutes, but I'm not really into it. Kevin's funeral is scheduled for Wednesday back in Brantford. Mom is picking me up Tuesday after she finishes work. Honestly, everything else seems stupid and vapid. But I can't sit there doing nothing. My eyes keep wandering back to the front door. I know it's locked, but my inner critic is whispering to me in a loop, urging me to check again and again. One of the benefits of living in a high-rise without an external fire escape is I never have to worry about people creeping in through my window. Otherwise I probably would have nailed the windows shut.

I turn off the PS4 and log onto my computer. All I care about now is Facebook. I have to know if Delilah responded. And there it is.

"I miss you, too. Please call me. I need to see you. Hugs."

And now I'm wishing I had a landline like my mom. I pull my phone out and try turning it back on with the power of my will. Sadly, I have not randomly developed superhero powers in the last few hours.

"Well, at least I know what I should do with my afternoon."

I put on a coat, grab my keys and head to the mall. Time to talk to my service provider about a replacement phone.

***

The guy at Telus looks at the cracked screen and whistles. "Looks like someone was having a bad day."

I groan and sit on one of those weird plastic bar stools they have. "You have no idea. But I bought that stupidly expensive insurance plan, so you should be able to get me a replacement phone, right? Any chance I can get a phone today?"

The guy nods, mumbling something as he wanders off. I'm barely listening to him because I'm starting to feel anxious again. The Telus store is nearly empty, but the mall is busy. It's a Saturday, only a few weeks before Christmas. I'm surrounded by strangers. I search for closed doors, but everything here feels so open. If a zombie invasion happened right now, we'd all be screwed.

Of course, I'm not really thinking about zombies. I'm looking for the most defensible place in case someone starts to chase me. In case I need a place to hide. But there is nowhere to hide. Even the employee area out back is only separated by a swinging door. No locks.

Something moves off to the left and I jump. It was a blip, so minor I could have imagined it, but it looked like someone ducked down behind the lottery booth just before my eyes could land on them. I stand, trying to get a better vantage point. I start to walk out of the store when I hear someone call my name.

It's the guy that works at Telus. He's got my new phone. He's handing me a box and some paperwork. After telling me the phone isn't fully charged, he also says they've transferred all the pictures and contact information to the new phone. All I care about is being able to call Delilah.

The back of my neck itches like someone is watching me again. I look around but can't find anyone looking in my direction.

I need to get out of here, back home where I can lock the front door and shut out the world.

Telus Guy is trying to get me to buy a protective case. I start to brush him off and tell him I'm not interested but stop, remembering who I am as a person. Given how often I think about throwing my phone, a protective case might be a good idea after all.

The first thing I do with my new phone is call a taxi. The way I'm feeling I'd rather not be on public transit.

***

When I get home, I triple check that the front door is locked. I change into sweatpants and an old t-shirt and dial Delilah's number. She answers on the second ring.

"Yes?" Hearing her voice makes me smile.

"Hey, D, it's me. Clive." I sit down on the couch, leaning forward. For some reason I'm a nervous wreck.

"Oh, Clive." She exhales slowly, and it makes me relax. It feels like she's hugging me with her voice. "I've been thinking about you a lot. How are you? I know it's a stupid question, but . . ."

"No. It's okay. Honestly? I don't know how I am. Guess everyone knows about this at work, eh?"

She tells me about the last few days at work. Yes, everyone knows what happened to me and Kevin. Reporters have shown up out in front of the building trying to interview anyone who might know me.

I can tell from her voice that Delilah is annoyed. "Creepy vultures. HR sent out a memo that told everyone to keep their mouths shut, but some people still blabbed. Thankfully, everyone said nice things about you. Even that bitch Rhoda."

"Rhoda said something nice? About me?" I laugh and lean back on the couch. "Is that even possible? Did the laws of physics stop working?"

She laughs back. There's a pause that is only slightly too long. "Do you mind if I come over?"

I hold my breath, thinking. "I . . . Christ. Yes. I mean no. I mean, I think I'd like that a lot. I'm over near Bloor and Islington. I'll text you my address, apartment number and buzz code. It's different than my apartment number because it's supposed to be more secure that way." I know I'm babbling, but the thought of seeing her away from work, seeing her here in my apartment, which just so happens to be attached to my bedroom, has me all kinds of wonky.

"I'll be there in half an hour," she says, "assuming traffic isn't horrendous. I'll bring wine."

This is such a bad idea. "Sounds great. I'll order pizza. See you soon."

As soon as I hang up, I look around and see that my apartment is a complete disaster. I can't even blame the police. I honestly can't recall the last time I cleaned. I order pizza from this little place in the nearby shopping plaza. It's a race against time to pretend I don't live like a Neanderthal. My dirty clothes get thrown into a closet. I empty the dishwasher and immediately refill it with a week's worth of dishes I've left in the sink. After that, I sweep and Febreze the fuck out of all my furniture. I also light every candle I have. I don't have time to wash my sheets, which still smell like Tonia. This is actually a good thing. Gives me another excuse to keep out of the bedroom. I do, however, empty the garbage bin to get rid of the old condom.

Glancing at my watch I see I've got about five minutes before Delilah could show. I sniff under my armpits and gag. Turns out racing around in a frenzy of cleaning is great cardio. Can't risk time for a shower so I throw my dirty shirt into the pile of other shirts hidden in the closet and quickly wash my armpits. I make the mistake of looking in the mirror.

I've mentioned that I'm built like a broom handle, right? In an age where the rest of the world is battling obesity, I can eat McDonald's daily and still look like this. My collarbones stick out farther than my nipples. Ick. They say your metabolism slows down around 24 or so. Here's hoping. My hair is also a complete disaster, so after I put on a Marilyn Manson t-shirt I throw on a baseball cap.

I'm in the middle of second-guessing my choice in t-shirts when the buzzer rings.

I may have squealed. Thankfully, the door is practically soundproof and . . .

Wait.

"If the doors are soundproof, how did Gabriel hear me and Kevin come in?" I stand there numb, running that over and over in my mind.

The buzzer rings again.

"Crap." The buzzer is one of those ancient types still mounted on the wall. I've heard most new ones go directly to your phone. I push the button to speak into the lobby. "Yes?"

"It's me, Clive." Delilah. I'm glad I'm not in front of a mirror anymore because I think I'm blushing again at the sound of her voice.

"Come on up." I push the button to let her in. As I'm waiting, all I can think about is how Gabriel said he heard me come in. The only way that makes sense is if he had his door open. Either that or the doors aren't as soundproof as I thought. I've never heard him come in. But maybe Kevin and me were just super loud. I mean I was drunk and . . .

There's a knock on the door.

For a second I hold my breath and panic. I slap my forehead repeatedly to snap out of it. I look through the peephole. And there she is. She's wearing a thick black jacket and a pink winter hat.

"Get it together, Clive." I open the door.

She smiles at me and I drink in every detail of her. Snowflakes melting on her shoulders. Her coat has a Roots label on it. Her black Doc Martins have traces of salt and snow along the bottoms. She's not wearing any makeup, but she smells good, something she's worn before. I think it's call Shi by Alfred Sung. Her lips are moist, and her skin is flushed from coming in out of the cold. She's holding a brown paper bag in both her gloved hands.

It isn't until she clears her throat and raises an eyebrow that I realize I've been staring at her for a while.

"Oh. Sorry." I step aside and motion for her to come in.

As the door swings closed, she passes me the brown paper bag.

"It's getting nasty out there again." She takes off her hat and gloves, putting them in her coat pocket. Then she's unbuttoning her coat to reveal an Alanis Morissette t-shirt. "Is there somewhere I can throw my coat?"

"I'll take it." The closet off my entrance is also a complete disaster. The less she sees of my mess the better. She slips out of her coat and hands it to me. I reach for it and our hands touch. She's standing so close to me. I know I need to take the coat, but I can't take my eyes off her.

"Um . . . pizza should be here in a few minutes. Did you have trouble–"

Delilah kisses me. At first, it's gentle, a small tenderness that sends shivers through me. I can't move. It's like those corny moments in movies when the whole world seems to stop, and there is just the two of us. She leans in farther and her hands are cupping my face. I feel myself open to her, and I'm instantly erect. I'm kissing her back. I drop her coat on the floor, and I'm pushing her back until she's up against the closed door. My hands are in her hair and I'm ready to give her everything.

The buzzer rings again.

"Leave it." Delilah moans. "We don't need pizza."

I leave her mouth and kiss the side of her neck. She moans and her hands reach for my waist.

The buzzer rings again. I take a step back. She moves to kiss me again and I hold her in place.

"Whoa," I say. "Maybe we should have pizza and talk about what this means before we . . . "

She puts her hand on my crotch. "We can talk later."

After that I don't hear the buzzer anymore.

**

Hours later, I wake up to the smell of bacon. I panic and look at my watch. Phew. It's not the morning, which means that's not breakfast. I never keep bacon in the house, which means this must be . . .

I sniff the air. "Pizza."

My bedroom is tossed. Sheets lie half on the bed, half on the floor. Delilah's socks are still near the door, but her clothes are gone. I get dressed and head to the living room. Delilah is pulling slices of steaming pizza from a box and putting them on plates.

"God, I think I love you." As soon as the words leave my mouth I panic. I feel like all the blood has left my face. "Wait, I didn't mean . . ."

Delilah is laughing and she passes me a plate. "I know what you meant. Relax, tiger. I figured you could use some refueling. Do you want to sit on the bed or the couch?"

"Couch." I take a bite of pizza. It tastes ridiculously good like I haven't eaten in days. "Not sure I trust myself anywhere near a bed right now. I know you're not supposed to say things like this, but damn, girl. You are most amazing. You know that thing you did with your tongue?"

She takes a bow. "What can I say? When I saw that monster I got inspired."

I follow her to the living room and for several minutes we eat in silence. It feels remarkable to be here with her like this. I haven't felt this comfortable with anyone in a long time. Possibly ever. I don't want to ruin anything, but I know we need to have a conversation. To figure out what this means. Delilah must know what I'm thinking, because her expression changes. She puts her pizza down and turns to face me.

I put my hand on her knee. "So where do we go from here?"

"I don't know. Isn't that part of the fun?" She touches my hand. "I like you, Clive. I have for a long time, probably longer than you know. This can mean whatever we want it to mean."

This feels like a trap. I know that girls say things like this, but what they mean is, "I want to be your girlfriend, but I want you to think I don't need to be your girlfriend, because if you know I want to be your girlfriend it means I lose control of the situation and you win."

If I say I'm cool being friends with benefits, that tells her she's not dateable and she will immediately hate me forever. If I say "Let's go out," I'm into her and I immediately lose control of the situation. Why can't anything ever be simple?

I sigh.

Fuck it.

"I want you, D. Not just the sex part – which was life-altering, by the way – but the whole thing. I want there to be a you and me. A thing. Not just a bumping and moaning thing, either. A best friend thing. A fairy tale thing. Maybe I'm a loser for being honest but . . ."

Her eyes are wide. "No. You're . . . I just wasn't . . ."

Crap. Did I go too far? If I scare her off, I don't know what I'll do.

Delilah leans in and kisses me. "You really aren't like other guys, are you?"

And there it is. I've accidentally opened myself too far. I can't be fake with Delilah. If I actually want a relationship with her, it means I have to start being honest. I need to tell her why I'm not like other guys.

Something must show on my face, because Delilah leans back. She's looking at me so closely it seems she can almost read my mind. She brushes hair off my forehead and for just a moment all I want to do is cry. I hear my dad's voice again. Man up. I pull away from Delilah a bit, and I can see she's disappointed. Fuck. This may be a record. It usually takes me a few weeks before I start disappointing people.

"Clive," she says. "Whatever's going on, you can tell me."

I snort. It's an angry sound. I know I'm being a jerk, so I take a deep breath. "I'm sorry. I'm not really good at this. Talking about feelings and crap. It should be easy, considering how much therapy I've been through."

"Therapy?" She's giving me that look again. "I take it this isn't about your friend Kevin."

I shake my head. My ears are tingling, and I feel the urge to clean them.

"You don't have to tell me anything you don't want to."

"But that's just it." I rub my ear and glance over towards the front door. "I do want to tell you. I'm scared. Terrified, actually. But I want us to be something real. I don't want secrets and I don't want to lie to you. I don't act like other guys because I'm not normal."

"Clive . . ."

"No. Let me get this out. Please. It's hard to talk about, but if we're going to do this thing, I want you to be in a relationship with me, not the guy I pretend to be all the time."

Delilah says nothing. She just listens, waiting for me.

"When I was twelve, something happened to me. One of the neighbors had a thing for young boys, and . . ."

Before you know it, the whole thing is spilling out. I can't look at her as I'm talking, but I can feel her presence. She's not running away, which is a good sign. It takes me over an hour, but I tell her the whole thing. The nail gun and the scars. How I was rescued and about the other boys who weren't so lucky. I talk about the years of going through the courts and endless therapy.

Despite what I said about being honest, there's still lots of stuff I don't tell her. I skip over why my parents put me in therapy. I went through a dark phase when I wanted to set everything on fire. Sometimes I burnt things, and they caught me. I also skip over the whole liking-to-jerk-off-in-public thing. Look, I know Delilah is amazing, but there's only so much you can expect a girl to swallow at one time. It hits me then and there I'm done with it. All of it. I can't be with her and post things online. I would literally die if she found out about them. Or worse, saw them.

When I finish, there's a period of silence. I'm done talking, and I know that Delilah has to say something. What she says next will determine our entire future. If she says the wrong thing, I'll never forgive her. Maybe that's unfair but it's the truth. I've laid my soul bare for her. I'm completely vulnerable. Men aren't supposed to be fragile and if she abuses my trust . . .

Turns out I had nothing to worry about. Delilah says the most perfect thing.

She grabs my hand and squeezes it lightly. "Clive, you are the bravest, strongest man I've ever met."

I snort again. I can't look at her because I know I'm crying.

"I'm serious. What you went through would destroy most. But look at you. No one would guess you've been carrying this . . . thing with you." She reaches down for my hand and kisses the scars. "You've been hurt so bad, and you are still so kind. Only a very strong person could do that."

I bite my lip. "I don't feel very strong." I can hear my father screaming at me. Man up, Clive. Man up. But Delilah makes me want to be soft. I shift on the couch, putting my head in her lap. She strokes my hair, and I want to feel at peace. But all the while my father's voice is screaming at me, judging me.

I wonder if I'll ever feel at peace.

CHAPTER FIFTEEN

After Delilah goes home, I slip into bed. The sheets smell of her now, and I don't feel so alone.

It's only later that I realize I was so relaxed I forgot to make sure the door was locked.

They say talking about stuff is supposed to be cathartic, like you can get it all out of your system or something. But all talking did for me was bring it all back.

My dreams are about the basement. I dream I'm bleeding, unable to move. Mitchell Baxter's muffled screams are all around me. I didn't know his name at the time. He came in after me. Unlike the others, he wasn't from the trailer park. He was just some kid a few years younger than me chained to the floor, the one with the missing tongue. Not missing. Sitting in a mason jar on a nearby shelf. I remember the tongue vividly. Seeing it is what kept me quiet.

In the dream, I feel my abductor approach me. I smell the dirty sweat and sickening cologne wafting off him. He whispers in my ear "Good boy. Pretty boy." And he's touching me. Then . . .

I wake up screaming. I sit up in bed breathing heavily. None of it was real. Just dreaming. I look over at the doorway and scream again.

A figure stands in the doorway. A man with something in his hand.

There's nowhere to run so I know I have to fight. I grab the first thing I can – a box of condoms – from my bedside table and whip it at him. He throws something back at me, and I roll off the bed before it can hit me. I close my eyes and flip on the light, hoping the sudden brightness will blind the intruder. Eyes still closed, I rush in the direction of the door, hoping to knock him over. My shoulder hits the door frame and I open my eyes. I see the man – a six-foot-tall slender figure in a black hooded coat – and now I'm more terrified than ever. I'd been clinging to the hope that the man wasn't really there, that what I saw was only the remnants of a dream.

As he throws open my front door, I focus on him, trying to take in as much information as I can. In court cases, eyewitness testimony isn't as reliable as you think. In the heat of the moment, people are too busy reacting to pay attention. So I force myself to stay calm and do my best to really see him as he's running out into the hallway. He's taller than me, wider in the shoulders. He's wearing a thick parka with the hood pulled up to obscure his face. He's wearing thin leather gloves, blue jeans, and big winter boots that look brand new, without any salt or snow stains. He's also much faster than me.

I chase after him. I'm in the hallway, but vaguely aware that I'm still naked. He throws open the door to the stairs. I'm about to rush after him when logic takes over. I'm being incredibly stupid. Why am I running after someone who could be a serial killer? I don't even have a weapon. I stop and head back to my apartment. Standing in the doorway, looking at my dark apartment a feeling comes over me. I can't go back in there. What if someone else is in there waiting for me?

Instinct tells me to run, but I need to get to my phone, to call the police before the intruder decides to come back. I'm shaking, and I can't do this alone. There's a closet just inside to the right. It's open slightly and my mind convinces me I hear breathing coming from inside it. Rationally, I know there isn't anyone there, but that part of my brain isn't in control right now. So, I do the only thing I can think of.

I hope I have a good neighbor.

Keeping one hand over my crotch, I knock on Gabriel's door. No answer. I wait for a bit and knock again, even louder. Still no answer.

Why isn't he home? Of course. It's Saturday night, and anyone with a social life is probably out enjoying themselves. He could also be sleeping. Or maybe he's not an idiot and knows you shouldn't answer your door in the middle of the night. I know I need help, and I'm about to pull the fire alarm when another thought comes to me.

Maybe Gabriel isn't answering because he was the one in my apartment.

I freeze and step away from his door. Could it be? I think back to what I saw of the guy and try to compare him with Gabriel. Could they be the same person?

Gabriel's door opens. He's standing there in a bathrobe. At first, he smirks at my nakedness. I guess he sees how terrified I am. He looks up and down the hallway and motions for me to get inside. I push him aside and lock the door.

"What—?"

I interrupt him. "Call the police. He was here."

"Who was here?" Gabriel looks groggy. I guess I did wake him up, after all. "What's going on, Clive? Do I even want to know why you're naked?"

"Someone was in my room. I woke up and—"

"Christ." Gabriel turns on a few lights. "Are you okay? Let me get you something to wear."

I'm nodding and doing my best to keep it together. "Thanks. But call the police first. The guy ran down the stairs, but I don't know if he's gone."

I stand by the front door, freezing, and trying to act comfortable. I'm suddenly very glad that Delilah didn't spend the night.

Gabriel comes back. He's wearing jeans and a white t-shirt now. One hand has his cell phone pressed to his ear. In the other is a pair of gray jogging pants and a matching sweatshirt. He hands them to me and I quickly turn my back on him to slip on the pants. The modesty is irrational, considering he's already seen me naked. But whatever.

"Yes. An intruder," Gabriel says. "Did I stutter? Get someone over here immediately." I assume he's talking to a 911 operator. I listen as he tells her about finding me in the hallway and what I said. His voice is tense and from the expression on his face it seems this isn't the first time he's told her these details. It seems like the person he's talking to isn't taking him seriously. Gabriel mentions my name and my connection to the recent killings. That seems to do the trick.

"Tell them to contact Detective Coyle," I say. "He's in charge of the investigation."

Gabriel nods and repeats what I said. I put on the sweatshirt and instantly feel a little better. Strange how a thin layer of clothing can make you feel stronger. Gabriel hangs up and gets this strange look in his eye. I don't like it.

"Stay here," he says. He unlocks the door.

"No! What the fuck are you doing? Don't go out there. For all we know—"

Gabriel puts a finger to his lips. "The police are on their way. I'm going to check your apartment. You said he threw something at you. I want to make sure he doesn't come back to get it."

Before I can stop him, he's out the door. I take one look at his dark apartment before following him.

He looks back at me, annoyed. "I told you to stay."

"And I told you not to leave. Looks like we're both ignoring each other. There's no way I'm staying anywhere alone right now."

Gabriel mumbles something under his breath. "Fine. Just remember I'm trained to deal with this. You're not."

I frown. "You're trained to deal with serial killers?"

Gabriel stops and throws his hands up in the air. "Do you seriously not know anything about me? What do I do for a living? I've told you at least five times."

"Um . . . " I shrug.

"Why do I even bother?" He shakes his head but, annoyingly, doesn't fill me in on what he does. I seriously need to get my memory checked because he's right. I know almost nothing about him. I don't even know Gabriel's last name. I think Amy mentioned it, but I forgot it immediately after she said it. And here I am heading back into my apartment with a complete stranger when there's a serial killer running around. How do I know he actually called the police? For all I know, he's working with the serial killer, trying to trick me into a false sense of security.

Standing in the doorway to my apartment, Gabriel flips on the light. He's got a weapon in his right hand. Some sort of metal rod thing.

"What kind of weapon is that?" I follow Gabriel into my apartment. Even though the lights are on, it no longer feels like a safe place. "Remind me what you do again?"

Gabriel waves his hand to hush me. "We'll chat later, buttercup. For now, shush up and watch my back."

"Did you seriously just call me 'buttercup'? You're the gay one, aren't you?"

Gabriel snorts. "Well, at least you remember something about me." He flicks his wrist and the metal thing extends a bit. It's kind of like a police baton but much thinner. "This is an asp baton. Technically, I'm not supposed to have it, so don't mention to the police when they show up, okay?"

"No problem." Since Gabriel won't tell me what he does, in my mind I've decided he's a ninja. Or maybe a hired assassin.

We check the whole apartment. It's empty. When we get to my bedroom, I see it lying there, the thing the intruder threw at me. It's a Lillie doll, naked with a noose around her neck and duct tape over her mouth.

"Christ." I feel woozy.

"I take it that's not yours." Gabriel slams the end of the metal rod against the outer concrete wall and it shrinks to a smaller size. He tucks the asp in the waist of his pants, like hoodlums do in the movies, and pulls his shirt over it to conceal it. He leans close to the doll lying on top of my bed. "This psycho is crazier than I thought. Is that a Barbie?"

I shake my head. "Close. It's a Lillie doll."

"Who breaks into someone's apartment to throw a doll at them?"

"Serial killers." My new phone is still in the pocket of my jeans which lie crumpled on the floor. I reach down and fish out the phone. It feels like a weapon. "What I don't get is why didn't he kill me?"

"Hmm. You're right. He should have killed you."

I smack Gabriel on the arm.

"Sorry. That came out wrong. I just meant what he did tonight doesn't fit the pattern." He leans over the doll, studying it. "I'm no doll expert, but something tells me these aren't standard-issue accessories. He's trying to send a message. Maybe it's to you. More likely he's hoping you'll report this to the press. Or someone else. We should wait in the hallway. Don't want the investigating unit to think we've interfered with the crime scene."

I follow Gabriel out into the hallway. "What are you? Some sort of cop?"

Gabriel crosses his arms and glares at me. "You know, normally people find me pretty memorable. At first I thought you had something against gay people, but . . ."

I sigh. "It's not you. Without getting into my life story, I have issues. There's a lot going on in my head, and sometimes I blank on people. Other things stick in my head easily. Like the security system you installed in your apartment. I can tell your password is four digits. Three, four, eight, and zero. I don't know what order they're in, but . . ."

Gabriel's eyes narrow. "How the hell can you possibly know that?"

"Grease marks. You don't clean your keypad often. Those numbers are a bit greasier than the others. I've learned to pay attention to the small things. It's usually the small things that come back to haunt you."

"Sometimes. Other times you get into trouble because you're not watching the big picture." Gabriel steps into his apartment. Once I'm inside he sets the alarm. "Guess I'll be changing my password tomorrow."

I follow Gabriel to the living room and my jaw drops. His furniture is all white leather and has that vague aroma of wealth that's hard to quantify, like something you'd find in a movie star's mansion. But that's not why my jaw drops. It's the pictures. There's an entire wall filled with poster-sized black and white photos of Gabriel with celebrities.

"Is that really Channing Tatum?" I'm leaning closer trying to see if it's real or Photoshop.

"Yep." Gabriel opens a crystal decanter and pours what I assume is scotch into two tumblers. He passes one to me and drinks from the other. "I've worked on a few pictures with him. Nice guy."

I'm really confused now. "So . . . you're an actor?" How can I not remember living next to a movie star?

He shakes his head. "Stunt man. TV shows, mostly, but I did quite a few movies when I lived in Vancouver."

"And that trained you to hunt serial killers?"

Gabriel frowns for a moment and looks away. "More than you might think."

"You must have some great stories to tell." I sip my drink and silently thank a dozen gods that it actually is scotch: Lot 40 by J.P. Wiser. One of the best in the world.

Gabriel shrugs. "Not really. Actors are just people. Some are nice. Others are dicks. My only cool stories are about traveling. Paris. Hong Kong. Gobekli Tepe. My job won't make me a millionaire, but I've been to some pretty amazing places." He finishes his drink, quickly refilling his glass. "You surprise me, Clive. Most people wouldn't be handling this as well as you. Finding a stranger watching them sleep . . . well, most people would be a puddle."

I stare down at my drink. "I'm not handling this well at all. I've just spent years learning how to pretend to be normal. I want to break down – trust me – but I can't afford to. Not right now. That will come later."

Gabriel finished his second drink. "Well, until then we have alcohol."

CHAPTER SIXTEEN

Twenty minutes later, I'm back in my apartment answering questions with Detective Coyle. My place is crawling with cops. Again. I have no idea what they're doing. Dusting for prints or something. Gabriel is on the balcony, smoking, as Coyle's partner interviews him. I still don't know her name. That sort of thing never used to bother me, but recent events drive home the fact that maybe I've been focusing my attention on the wrong things. I need to start paying attention.

I clear my throat. "Detective Coyle, what's your partner's name? I don't think I caught it."

"Oh?" He looks confused for a second and then glances towards the balcony.

"Me and people's names have a pretty distant relationship."

Coyle smiles. "No worries. Her name's Demena. Detective Demena. Understandable. You've had a lot going on these last few days. As I was saying, the first thing we checked was the front door. No sign of forced entry. Now, picking locks isn't as common a skill as they make it look like in the movies. So on a hunch, I checked with maintenance when I got here. The management company keeps copies of keys to all apartments in case of emergencies. Broken pipes and whatnot. Just so happens, yours is missing."

"Wait." I hear something in his voice that sets me on edge. "You think this person could live here? A tenant in this building?"

"Tenants don't have access to keys. But maintenance would." He frowns and puts his notepad away. "Of course, this is nothing but speculation. Thankfully, you live in a secured building so there's video for us to check. We'll know who's had access to the keys. It could just as easily be someone with a relation to the locksmith who changed the lock. But someone who lives in this building? That would explain a few things. Like how he got away so quickly. My money says he knows where the cameras are. That's likely how he was able to get Kevin out."

I remember a little thing and hold up my hand. "His boots. There was no salt on them. I had a friend come by earlier. Her boots had salt stains. If you look, I'm betting you'll find they recently salted the parking lot."

Coyle gives me a slow blink. "Damn. That gives credence to the idea the intruder lives here. His shoes didn't have salt stains because he didn't go outside. Or, it could mean he treated the shoes to prevent that kind of damage. Or maybe there really were salt stains, but they were faint and you didn't see them. Sometimes you can't trust your eyes, Mr. Dufault." He sighs, looking very tired. "Now to the big question. Why do you think this person is fixated on you?"

I open my mouth to answer but end up just shaking my head.

Coyle leans forward, lowering his voice. "Is it possible this is connected with your incident? The thing that happened to you as a child."

I shrug, feeling uncomfortable. "I don't see how. The guy is still in jail."

"Are you sure?"

Now I feel exposed and horrified. "Christ. I think so. I think I would know if he was released. Wouldn't I? I think they inform the families or something. His name's Banner. Zacharia Banner. You mean you didn't look into it?"

Coyle looks annoyed. "Nah. Maybe not the smartest decision on my part, but you didn't think it was related, and we had so many other leads. Maybe this Banner has a family member or friend that blames you for his incarceration and wants revenge."

"That's not creepy at all." I scratch my jaw. My skin feels like things are crawling on me. "I only remember his mother from the trials. I think she's the only support he ever had. Thankfully, not many people want to be seen supporting a child-killer."

Coyle flinched.

"Sorry." It feels like greasy, gray goo is swimming up my throat and I want to vomit. "Guess I skipped that part. Banner took eight boys. Only three of us made it."

"Jesus." Coyle rubs the back of his neck. "Banner. Wait. Banner worked for the Department of Parks and Rec, right? I think I remember the case now. About eight years ago, right? One of the dead boys had his tongue . . . um . . ."

I wince. "That's the one. Joy of joy."

Coyle takes out his notepad again and scribbles a few notes. "I'll look into it. Make sure this guy Banner is still locked away. I'll also check on the other survivors. See if they've experienced anything similar. Can you think of anyone else that would want to target you?"

"I have no flippin' idea." My hands are shaking, so I stick them under my legs, sitting on them. "Up until tonight I didn't think he was focused on me. I thought it was about those videos I sent you. He was after people who refused to play his game." Something else comes to mind. "Before I forget, there are a few other things. The day before he was killed, Kevin told me there was something going on at his workplace. He found a file he shouldn't have found, and his boss suddenly disappeared. You should look into that."

Coyle scribbles a few more notes. "Hmm. Anything else?"

I tell him about the pictures Kevin sent me of that girl, the ones he denied sending. I show him the pictures on my phone and promise to email them to him later. He says he'll look into it, make sure the girl is okay.

A horrible thought is forming in my head. Maybe it wasn't the video or anything with to do with his work. Maybe the only reason Kevin is dead is because of me. I don't want to go anywhere close to following that train of thought, so I change gears.

"So what's up with the doll?"

"It's . . . peculiar." Coyle scrubs his chin where the beginnings of whiskers are growing. "We've kept it out of the papers, but we've found similar dolls at each previous crime scene. That info is strictly need-to-know, so . . ." He puts his finger in front of his lips, motioning for silence.

"Can't you track down purchases of the type of doll or something?"

Coyle gives me another slow blink. "Gee. Why didn't I think of that?" He flips some pages in his notebook. "Interesting fact. According to the company's website, a Lillie is sold every three seconds. They've sold something like a billion since it launched. Each doll we've found has been modified slightly . . . but I'm afraid I'm not at liberty to discuss the details."

"Seriously?" For a second I want to strangle him. "You found the thing in my freakin' bedroom. Doesn't that put me in the need-to-know category?"

Coyle lowers his eyes and frowns at me. So I try a different tactic.

"Besides, if you tell me, maybe it will click something for me. If I know, I could help you . . ."

Coyle holds up his hand to stop me. "I'll ask if you can be brought into the loop. But there's a chain of command here, son."

Wonderful. I remember something else. "Did you have any luck tracking down that guy Matt Elliott? He was a fan of one of my videos. If he's actually the same guy who taped the other videos, maybe . . . I don't know. Maybe he feels we have a connection. Like because he's a voyeur and I'm . . ." I flounder for the word. What am I? A freak who gets off having sex in public.

"The term we use is exhibitionist," Coyle says.

I nod. "Sure. That works better than what I was thinking. Maybe because I like being seen he . . . I don't know. Does that make any sense?"

"Maybe. People who kill usually have their own type of logic." Coyle's eyes narrow and he looks away. ""We checked the profile you sent us. I expected it to be deleted, but either Elliott isn't our guy, or he isn't very smart. According to his profile he liked lots of videos."

"So why isn't he targeting anyone else?" I exhale slowly and run my hands through my hair. "Because maybe he's not targeting anyone. Maybe he has nothing to do with this."

Coyle sighs and looks even more tired than before. "We're checking all possible leads. Tracking down the real people behind online personas is much harder than people think. Mostly because of staffing limitations, honestly. We're still working on it, but with getting warrants and following proper procedure . . . Hopefully we'll know something in a few weeks."

"A few weeks. Jesus. He could kill a ton of people by then."

Coyle grimaces. "You're preaching to the choir. We've tracked the last IP address used to access the account, but that's likely a dead end."

"How so?"

"Last location was in a Korean Barbecue restaurant on Queen Street. We checked. They have no security cameras. Their wifi isn't password protected. The signal could easily have been hijacked from across the street."

"Any video surveillance?"

He shakes his head. "Active security cameras are actually pretty rare. Half the time you see a camera installed it's not connected to anything. Or they only record when the business is closed. Even if they do record something, odds are pretty good they only keep a few days of video on file. I tell you, my job would be a heck of a lot easier if police departments really had the resources you see on NCIS. We've interviewed the staff and we're checking out a few of their regulars, but . . . my gut tells me that's not how we're going to find him."

Detective Demena comes over and whispers something in Coyle's ear.

He nods and turns back to me. "We're almost done here. We'll keep a unit out front tonight in case the intruder comes back. That's not likely, but . . . you never know. I've put in a request for a protective detail, however . . ." He hangs his head. "Best thing for you, find someplace else to stay for the time being. I'll have a unit take you to a hotel for the night if you want. After that, maybe you should consider staying with your parents."

"Christ. I can't. I have a job and . . ." Another bad thought comes to mind. "If it isn't this Matt Elliott guy, if it's someone connected to my past, he'll know where my parents live. I don't know what I'd do if anything happened to them."

Gabriel comes over and looks at Coyle. "I've got a place he can stay."

My eyes go wide. "Really? You're offering me your couch?"

He shakes his head. "No. One of my buddies is out west in Vancouver working on a movie. He's not back in Toronto for a few months."

"Won't he mind?" I ask. "Don't get me wrong. Sounds perfect to me. If I'm being stalked, the apartment of a random dude I have zero connection to sounds ideal. I should be impossible to find."

Gabriel shakes his head. "He owes me one. There are two guest bedrooms. I'll pack a bag and stay with you. I'm guessing you won't mind the company."

The image of the shadowy figure standing in my doorway pops up in my mind again. "No. I won't mind the company at all. I've got the week off work, but I have to go to Kevin's funeral in a few days. What if he follows me back?"

Coyle puts his hand on my shoulder. "Look around you. Do you think there would be this many police officers here if we didn't care about your safety? For whatever reason, you are our strongest link to the killer."

"So, we're certain the intruder was the Plastic Strangler?" Gabriel asks.

Coyle nods. "I wasn't sure before, but the doll confirms it. It follows the pattern and only the killer would know."

Another thought occurs to me. "Or he could be a police officer."

Coyle puts his note pad away. "Mr. Dufault, I think you watch too much TV. You'll be protected at the funeral. I'm sure we can arrange something with the Brantford police. I'll drive you myself if necessary. My suggestion? When you get to this place Gabriel is taking you, stay there. Stay inside, stay out of sight and don't tell anyone except your mother where you are. Since this isn't a Wes Craven movie, I'm sure we can rule your mother out as a suspect."

Perfect, I think. A reference to the original Scream movie. Apparently Detective Coyle is a horror fan. Does that make him a suspect?

My entire world feels like it's spinning away from me. Just like before. My ears start to itch, and I would do anything to take a shower. I look around my living room. Everything is a mess. It looks familiar but distant, like a model apartment instead of a home.

"Fine," I say. "I'll go pack a few bags."

Gabriel puts his hands behind his back, a movement that for some reasons reminds me of the military. "I'm going next door to do the same. Let me know when you're ready."

When Gabriel leaves, Coyle stands and passes me a business card. "I've written my home number and my cell on the back. Call me any time of day or night. I'll have a car follow you tonight to make sure you get there safe. I know it will be hard but try to get some sleep tonight."

I stand and head to my bedroom, not sure what other choice I have. I'm pushing past strangers who are all over my apartment. The doll is still on my bed. People are taking pictures of it from all angles. I watch as they place the doll in a see-through evidence bag. Something about it doesn't sit right with me, something familiar, but I can't quite put my finger on it. Coyle was right, the features have been altered but I can't get close enough to see how.

I grab the bottle of valerian root and my sleep headphones, but just looking at them I wonder if I'll ever sleep again.

CHAPTER SEVENTEEN

The sun's edging up on the horizon by the time Gabriel pulls up to his friend's apartment building. I'm exhausted, barely conscious, so I'm not very clear on the address. I text Delilah because it's too early to call.

Something happened last night, after you left. Totally messed up but I'm okay. Call me when you're up and I'll explain.

I put my phone away as Gabriel pulls the car up to the underground parking security point and rolls down the window. He swipes a white card across the metal scanner, and the heavy garage door opens. We drive down a ramp into the darkness of underground parking. I look over my shoulder. The police car that has escorted us here does not follow us down.

Gabriel sees me looking. "Don't worry. Remember what Detective Coyle said."

I nod and remain silent as he turns the car around tight corners, each revolution bringing us down deeper and deeper. It's just after seven in the morning on a Sunday, so it's pretty empty. I see only a few people getting into their cars, likely heading to work.

Coyle told me there would be a unit at my old apartment, waiting in case the intruder returned again. He'd keep a car by this condo until we were secured in the apartment. As soon as we were settled, I was to text him with the okay. After that, we'd be on our own.

Gabriel parks the car and we get out. He presses a button on the key fob, and the door locks with a loud beep that echoes throughout the garage. Even though it's morning, and I know there are people all around me, I feel anything but safe. I have no idea where the exits are, and everything smells dirty and damp.

We unload our luggage and head to the elevator, which, thankfully, isn't far from our parking spot. Parking garages have always given me the creeps. I'm not sure why, but they always remind me of graveyards, like at any moment the dead are going to spring to life.

Gabriel presses his swipe card against a metal tray and the button for "penthouse" lights up automatically.

"Geesh," I say. "Guess this is one of your rich friends."

"He's got a few bucks," Gabriel says. "Just do me a favor and don't take pictures of his place. I don't think he'll mind us staying here under the circumstances, but he'll want to make sure nothing ends up on TMZ."

I have a weird feeling. "Just who exactly is this friend of yours?"

Gabriel shakes his head. "Nuh-uh. Not telling. Please don't go snooping, either. My friend is very particular about his privacy."

The elevator doors open to a short hallway with four doors. Gabriel takes out his keys and opens the last door on the left. Inside, on the righthand wall, a green light flashes on a black panel.

"Give me a second to disarm the security." Gabriel steps inside. He puts his back between me and the box, so I can't see which buttons he pushes. A few seconds later, I hear a long beep and Gabriel flicks on the lights. Immediately, I feel out of place.

The front door opens to an honest-to-goodness foyer the size of my entire apartment. I look up at the massive skylights. The condo appears to have three floors. Directly opposite the entrance is a wall of windows offering a panoramic view of Toronto.

Gulp. "I feel like I have to shower before I touch anything."

"I know. It's a little over the top. First floor is the living room and kitchen. Second floor has the pool table, bar and the guest bedrooms. Third floor is off limits, just the master bedroom and the TV room. Here, I'll show you your room."

Past the foyer is a spiral staircase that leads to the second floor. As soon as we start climbing, my phone rings. My hands are full with luggage, so I'll have to check it later.

On the second floor, Gabriel reaches into a dark room and flicks on a light.

"Jesus," I say. "This looks like Martha Stewart exploded all over the place." The bed has like a gazillion silk pillows on it. The outside wall is again one great big window. The floor to ceiling vertical blinds are tilted open, giving me an impressive view of the city. "All kidding aside, I could really use a shower."

"No problem." Gabriel walks past the bed and pushes open the door to what I had assumed was the closet. Only it turns out to be an ensuite bathroom. "Towels are inside. I'll leave you to it. I'll be in the room next door trying to get some sleep. I suggest you do the same. It's been a hell of a night."

After Gabriel leaves, I feel antsy. I want to shower but I don't feel safe enough to get naked. I lock the bedroom door, close the blinds, and head to the bathroom. I lock that door, too. Only then do I start taking my clothes off. I throw my shirt on the sink counter when I feel my phone buzz again.

"Crap." I check the number. Delilah. Both times. I hit the answer button and put the phone to my ear. "Hey, D. Sorry I didn't answer before. It's been crazy."

So, I tell her.

Once the story's over, I'm naked, sitting on the toilet. I keep one eye on the doorknob to make sure no one takes me by surprise. I tell her about Gabriel and this place he's taken me to. She asks where I am, and I tell her I honestly have no clue. Somewhere downtownish. I know there are thirty floors and my apartment faces northwest.

"I'm just glad you're okay," she says. From the sounds she's making over the phone, my guess is she's cooking breakfast.

I shake my head. "I just wish I understood why this was happening to me. I know the way my brain works. I won't be able to really shut it down until I understand why the killer is after me. Where's Veronica Mars when you need her?"

"Ah." Her voice seems to coo. "You, too, are a marshmallow. You just won major brownie points, mister. Get some sleep. I'll text you when I get home. Maybe we can Skype or something. Miss you."

I'm smiling as I hang up and place the phone on the counter. In case you didn't know, marshmallow is a term for fans of Veronica Mars, which I think we've established is my favorite show ever. It's been a long time since I've missed anyone. And maybe I'm being stupid, letting my emotions run too quickly and all because of how hectic life has been. But I really miss Delilah, too.

I double-check to make sure the door is locked and take a shower. I clean my ears, slip into a t-shirt and pair of jogging pants, and crawl into the ginormous bed, pushing aside half the pillows. I expect to lie awake as my brain loops recent events but, surprisingly, I pass out quickly.

**

Hours later, I wake up. Orange light peaks between the blinds. I check the time on my phone. It's nearly five. Aside from the ever-present faint rumble of traffic, the room is quiet. Peaceful. After hitting the bathroom, I unlock the bedroom door and step into the hallway. I hear sounds of dishes clinking and water running. I follow the sounds to the kitchen. Gabriel's there wearing the same thing he wore last night, cooking.

"You hungry?"

I nod and walk, zombie-like, to a bar stool by the marble-top island. "What time is it?"

"Almost five. You slept most of the day, which is good. You like spaghetti?"

"Of course." I yawn. "Never trust anyone that doesn't like spaghetti. Or pizza. Only communists don't like pizza."

Gabriel opens the fridge and pulls out two bottles of Alexander Keith's. He opens both and places one in front of me. He must see the hesitation on my face because he pushes the bottle closer to me.

"I don't want to hear it," he says. "Technically, this is your breakfast but it's evening and I hate to drink alone."

I shrug. "What the heck." Both of us are silent for a bit as we drink. Gabriel stirs his pasta sauce and grates cheese for some homemade garlic bread. Once the bread is in the oven, I clear my throat to get his attention.

"Say, can I ask you something?" I ask

"Shoot."

"I'm not exactly Mr. Sensitive, so let me know if this is out of line. Are the police really homophobic or is that complete bull?"

Gabriel takes a long swig of his beer before answering. "Mostly bull. At least, I like to think so. In my experience, police officers are just people. They're no more prejudiced or racist than anyone else. Having said that, the relationship between the gay community and the police has, historically, been pretty shitty. Many in my community aren't willing to let go of that. And maybe the police aren't doing as much as they should to acknowledge the past abuse. Have you ever been to the Pride Parade?"

"Well, yeah. Sure. Half the city goes to that."

"Nowadays, Pride is just a great big party." He leans against the fridge and looks at the beer bottle in his hand. "But it started as a political protest. Somehow, we've forgotten that. Back in February 1981, the police raided four bathhouses—"

"What's a bathhouse?" I ask.

Gabriel grimaced and shook his head slightly. "It's like a mix of a semi-private spa, a sex club, and a cheap hotel. Members pay a nominal fee, take off their clothes near the entrance, and walk around with towels around their waists. They wander around common rooms until they find a willing partner, then head to private rooms for sex."

"Do they have those for straight people?"

Gabriel blinks. "How would I know? Bathhouses aren't my scene. I don't see the need for them anymore, to be honest. Nowadays, we have phones apps for casual sex. Back then, it was different. Bathhouses were one of the few places you could go to meet other gay guys and not worry about being arrested, beat up or killed. Police monitored gay bars. It wasn't unheard of for them to find out where you work, call your boss and get you fired. You had to be anonymous if you wanted to survive."

"Jesus."

"I know, right? Anyway, there was this big raid. Something like two hundred cops armed with sledgehammers and crowbars swarmed four bathhouses. They knocked down the doors to private rooms and took pictures of the naked men for evidence. Cops smashed heads against the wall, broke noses, choked them, called them queers and fairies. Everyone had room numbers written on their backs or hands in permanent marker, the kind that doesn't wash off. They were forced to give the names and numbers of their employers and information on their immediate supervisors. Many were married to women. They were forced to give their wives names and numbers.

"Men found in the shower were lined up and told to face the wall with their arms up for over an hour while listening to cops joke about how they wished the pipes were hooked up to gas. Others were taken, still naked to holding areas. If they asked for their clothes, they were told to bend over and spread their cheeks while cops laughed. If they refused, they were hit.

"After they were arrested, their names and pictures were all over the TV and in the paper. It was seen as a deterrent, so other gays would think twice before going to the bathhouse. Of the hundreds arrested, only about six people had any charges stick to them. The rest of the charges were dropped. But it was too late. Lives were ruined. People lost jobs. Others were kicked out of their homes. A few committed suicide."

"You're shitting me."

Gabriel shakes his head. "Different time. Not that there's any shortage of assholes today, but I like to think we're evolving. Bigotry is the exception, now, not the rule. In a large part, it's because of Operation Soap and how the community responded. They were angry, and that anger brought them together. They took to the streets and stopped hiding. In a way, it's a lot like the Black Lives Matter movement you see in the United States. A group of oppressed people stood up and said, 'No More.'"

"How have I never heard of this before?"

Gabriel finished his drink and sets the bottle down. "It was before you were born. And you're straight. To be honest, even most gay guys don't know about the raids. They're too busy tweeting about RuPaul's Drag Race."

"Who's RuPaul?"

Gabriel rolls his eyes. "Wow. I'm going to pretend I didn't just hear that." He turns back to the stove, dumps spaghetti noodles from a big pot into a colander.

I literally have no idea who RuPaul is, but I let it go. The oven timer dings, and he takes the cheesy garlic bread out. The air fills with the smell of garlicy goodness, and I start to salivate. It seems like forever since my last meal. I want to forget everything and eat, but there's an important question I need to ask before I can relax. I'm starting to think Gabrielle might be an okay guy, but I don't want to let down my defenses too soon.

So, I clear my throat again and ask the question.

"How did you hear me come home?"

Gabriel stops arranging the cheesy bread on a platter and looks over at me.

I look away, nervous, but I can't stop. I have to know. "It's just . . . the fire doors are so thick. I never hear anything in the hallway, and . . ."

"You seriously don't know?" He's giving me this weird look now. With a sigh, Gabriel uses a pair of forks to dish the spaghetti out onto black ceramic plates. "You're right. The doors are thick and normally they block out everything. But you were . . . loud. I don't sleep much these days. I was in my kitchen when I heard singing. Then it turned to something else. Shouts."

I frown. "Shouts? What, like, I was yelling or something?"

Gabriel shakes his head. "Not you. I didn't recognize the voice. I assume it was your friend. I recognized your voice, though, when you started yelling back. I almost opened my door to see what was going on, but then it stopped. I guess you went into your apartment or decided whatever you were fighting about wasn't that important."

I'm confused. "I fought with Kevin?" Gabriel must have told this to the police. No reason he wouldn't. And if they police knew, maybe they said something to Jay. Now it makes sense why he confronted me, why he had to ask if I killed Kevin.

"More like he was trying to pick a fight with you. I couldn't catch most of it, but I do remember a word. Shinonach. Does that mean anything to you?"

I shake my head and reach for my beer before seeing that it's empty. Gabriel opens the fridge and gets me another one. He ladles sauce over each pile of pasta and puts one in front of me. He takes a seat on the opposite side of the island.

"Not even a little. Sounds Japanese. Like something out of an anime." I take a swig of the beer before I start eating. Not a good sign. I take a bite of the pasta and it's unbelievably good. "Whoa. Guess gay guys really do know how to cook."

He groans. "My mother's Italian, asshole. Being gay has nothing to do with it. So, you don't recall the fight?"

"Kevin and I never fought." I search my memory, but it's honestly all a blank. "We were drunk. What you heard is probably us just being loud and stupid. Maybe Shinonach is some type of beer. Or a new shot. I remember there were many shots."

"Maybe." Gabriel does not look convinced. "Anyway, the fight didn't last long. I probably would have forgotten about it completely except that cop was asking questions."

"Did you Google it?"

Gabriel shakes his head. "Nah. But I kind of want to now." He puts down his fork and takes out his phone. I hear him mumble beneath his breath as he's looking up the word. "Well, unless my spelling is wrong, Shinonach is the name of a major exporter of plastics and machinery."

"Let me guess. The headquarters is in Guangzho."

Gabriel nods and puts his phone down.

"So, that must be the company he found out about," I say. "The one who had the big explosion that killed all those people."

Gabriel picks up his phone again and types something in. "Huh. I typed in 'Shinonach explosion.' Nothing is coming up. Maybe it didn't make the news here."

"Or maybe it's been covered up." I realize I'm chewing with my mouth open and feel like a loser. So, I finish chewing and put my fork down. "But why would Kevin . . .?"

I don't even have to finish the sentence. I already know why Kevin would get in my face, yelling that company's name.

Gabriel is waving a hand in front of my face. "Where'd you go? Lost you for a second."

I chug the rest of my second beer. "Fuck. I think I made a connection. That's what I was missing before. Family. The coincidence is a little too convenient. I don't believe in coincidence. My father worked in Guangzho. What do you want to bet the police have not investigated the work history of the parents of the victims?"

Gabriel's eyes narrowed. "So, you think you're being targeted because your father worked for this company? Like this might be about revenge for something that happened there?"

For a moment, I just sit there, stunned. I shrug and pick up my fork again. "Who the hell knows? At first I thought it was my sex tapes."

Gabriel coughs like he's choking, and it hits me what I've just said.

I wince and slowly look away. "Long story. But maybe it has nothing to do with that. Maybe the first three victims being gay was just coincidence, or a distraction." The spaghetti is too good to let it get cold. When I've swallowed again, I continue. "If this is a revenge killing thing, the killer might be trying to throw people off his trail. Maybe he only wants us to think it's a gay thing."

Gabriel nods. "Or maybe you need to start taking your meds."

I blush. "How did you know I used to take meds?"

Gabriel laughs and finishes his beer. "I didn't. Until just now. It's a saying, Clive. Like something you say when the person you're talking to starts to sound a little crazy. So, who would the killer be? A family member of someone who died in the explosion?"

"Maybe. Or maybe someone who knows about the cover up and isn't happy. And yes, I said there's a cover-up. Kevin said people died in the explosion. Something like that should have made international news, right? Maybe the only reason it didn't is because someone paid for the story to disappear. This is a long shot but try Googling Shinonach and Toronto. What do you come up with?"

Gabriel punches something into his phone and flips through several screens. He finds something and reads it silently as I finish my meal.

He lowers the phone slowly and chews on his lower lip. "This can't be right."

"What can't?"

He passes me the phone. I read an article on the CBC news site. The article is almost a year old and discusses the ramifications for the Canadian auto industry of strengthening our ties with China. It discusses a convention of Chinese manufactures that took place in Toronto and features a few pictures.

"What am I looking at?"

"Look at the names," Gabriel said.

Ah, so I did miss something. It lists the names of five people on Shinonach's board of directors. Three of them are Chinese – Zhang Jindong, Shih Kien, Yuen Siu-tien. The other two, Lucius Vitalli and Otto Wiebe, are American. Vitalli sounds vaguely familiar, but the other names mean nothing to me. I shake my head and look up. Gabriel is pacing now.

"She said her uncle was in town," he says. "She was on the phone with him that night at the restaurant. I had no idea." He stops pacing. "Maybe it's nothing." He points a finger at me. "You're making me act like a crazy person."

I hold up my hands. "Whoa, I have nothing to do with this manic episode. Who are you talking about?"

He puts his hands on the island and leans forward. "Amy. Amy Vitalli. That man, Lucius, is her uncle."

And it clicks. "Damn. I didn't make the connection. I really need to start paying attention to people's names. But Amy can't be the killer? I saw the guy in my room."

"Are you sure it was a guy?"

I hesitate. "He smelled of Old Spice deodorant and he was way taller than Amy. Definitely not her. But she could be working with someone. We need to call the police."

"Hold up!" Gabriel's voice is sharp and loud. I've obviously missed something. He's visibly afraid. And hurt. "Amy is my friend. We've been friends for years. Let me talk to her first, before we bring this to the police."

I sit back and fold my arms. "Now who's the one not taking their medication? You can't confront a potential serial killer. That's how people end up dead."

Gabriel scoffs. "In the movies. I'm trained for this sort of thing."

"You've said that before. Tell me, how exactly does being a stunt man train you for police work?" Something else clicks. "Unless . . . you were on the force before you got into the movies, weren't you?"

He waves my sentence way. "Something like that, but it's not important right now." He runs to the wall and grabs his keys. "Stay here. I'm going to check Amy's place."

"Are you serious? That may be the worst idea in human history."

He grabs his coat and opens the door. "She's my friend. What would you do if you thought Kevin was mixed up in something? Would you turn him in?"

And there you go. Logic. Of course I wouldn't turn over Kevin, not for any reason. "Fine. But get out of there at the first sign of anything weird. I'm going to call my mom. Maybe she has records that can confirm my dad worked for Shinonach. You're right about one thing. Maybe we are seeing connections that don't exist. If we go to Coyle without proof, he'll just brush us off."

And I realize something else. I really do like Gabriel and don't want him dead.

"Be careful out there," I say.

He nods and makes his exit. The condo's silence is oppressive when he leaves. So, I grab another beer from the fridge and call my mother.

CHAPTER EIGHTEEN

Mom picks up on the third ring. I ask her where my dad worked when he was in Guangzho. Of course, she has zero memory of that. After several minutes of pleading, I convince her to look through some old paperwork for proof. After that, she asks me what's going on. I haven't told her about the incident at my apartment. For a nanosecond I think of lying to her, telling her everything is fine, so she doesn't worry. But that's the sort of lie that could come back to bite me.

So, I tell her. After she stops screaming, I convince her not to drive to Toronto to get me. I tell her the police have me somewhere safe, which isn't totally a lie. Eventually, I get her to calm down and we chat about Kevin's funeral. I tell her nothing in the world will keep me from it.

I hang up and, once again, feel like I'm drowning in silence. I sit on a couch in the living room looking out on the lights of the city. My mind is racing but my body feels numb. And I have the overwhelming urge to clean my ears.

I nearly run to my room and pull out my Q-tips. Once my ears are cleaned, I feel better.

Could Amy really be mixed up in all of this? Does that even make sense? She came to me with proof of a connection between the victims. Why would she do that if she was involved?

I open the browser on my phone and Google Lucius Vitalli. Almost nothing comes up, which is strange. If he's really a powerful businessman, why doesn't he have a Wikipedia page? All I see is a black and white photo of some blond guy getting into a limo, attached to an article about something called Bildenberg. He's also referenced on a website by David Icke, who claims Lucius is a shapeshifting lizard from the center of the earth.

"Well, now I feel less crazy." I search for Amy Vitalli and find tons of images. Amy's on Facebook and Instagram. I flip through her vacation pictures, shots of her out dancing with friends. There's even several of her with Gabriel. The most recent one on Instagram is only a few days old, a nice selfie featuring both of them walking through the snow, Christmas lights in the background.

I close the browser and head back to the kitchen to grab my unfinished beer.

I want to drink until I'm completely numb. I can't believe I let this happen again. When I was a kid, I lived close to someone who turned out to be a monster. And history just repeated itself. I let Amy into my life. She was tied up with the killer and I missed it. I've been training myself to pay attention to the little things. Make sure the door is locked. Count the exits. But by focusing on the small things I missed so many big things. I should have recognized the connection between their names immediately.

I think back to that incident on the subway when I had the panic attack. I remember the man with strawberry-blond hair who seemed to be looking at me. He looked familiar, but I couldn't place him. The black and white picture of Lucius Vitalli was pretty grainy, but I'm certain he wasn't the guy on the subway. That guy was in his mid-twenties. Maybe he was the killer. If I'd been able to pinpoint where I knew him from, maybe I would have been able to send the police after him. I needed to get better at paying attention to people. If the last few days have taught me anything, it is this: locking doors won't keep you safe. Paying attention will.

I leave my empty bottle on the counter. I look around. I still haven't scoped the place out. Gabriel told me the third floor was off-limits. So that's where I start.

I flick on the light switch and my eyes go wide. Most of the top floor is one large, open room. At the far end is a king-size bed with a white duvet and several large pillows. In one corner is a treadmill and a weight set. In another, red plush furniture in front of a fireplace. But it's the wall of pictures that floors me.

They're all celebrities. Candid photos of celebrities drinking and hanging out together placed in frames, the way you would place pictures of your closest friends. And the celebrity in almost everyone one of the pictures is Keanu Reeves.

"No way." I look around the room. Was I standing in Keanu Reeves' condo? "I fucking hate Keanu Reeves."

No, seriously, I do. Anyone that knows me can tell you that. I've given lectures about how much I despise his acting. So if Gabriel and he are friends, does that mean I have to stop hating him?

My phone rings. I feel guilty about trespassing, so I flip the light off and head back to the second floor before answering. It's Coyle.

"Good," he says. "You're safe."

"Why wouldn't I be safe? What's going on?" The condo is feeling big and vulnerable again.

"I'm here with Gabriel. We're at your apartment building looking for Amy. She's gone."

"Gone? Wait, did Gabriel call you?"

Coyle mumbles something. "No. I ran into him in the lobby. He's being questioned right now on Amy's disappearance. Anything you'd like to share?"

So, I tell him. Coyle lets out a long low whistle and puts me on speakerphone so his partner can hear. Both ask me questions, and I tell them everything I know, which honestly isn't much. Coyle tells me Amy's place was trashed, just like

Kevin's. There is no sign of blood and no Lillie doll, but it doesn't appear that she left voluntarily. As he talks, I go to the front door and makes sure it's locked. Thankfully, there's even a chain I can put over the door. No one is sneaking in here.

"We'll look into the parents," Coyle's partner says. Damn. Have I seriously forgotten her name again? Wait. It's Demena. Detective Demena.

"Are you alright on your own for a bit?" Detective Demena asks. "We need to take Gabriel down to the station, ask him more questions. It's going to take a few hours at least."

I nod, but remember I'm on the phone. "Sure. This is last place anyone would look for me."

"That's what Gabriel said, too," Coyle says. "He assures us that Amy doesn't know the location of that condo, but she is aware Gabriel is housesitting for a friend. If she shows up or attempts to contact you, do not let her in. Notify us immediately."

"Don't worry," I say. "I'm scared enough right now I wouldn't let Keanu Reeves into this place."

"Um . . . what?"

I shake my head. "Never mind. If Amy comes here, I'll let you know."

I hang up and check all the locks on the front door. I head back to the kitchen. I open the fridge, grab two beers and head back to my room. I call Delilah.

I spend the next hour telling her everything that's happened. The possible connection between the victims and Amy's potential involvement. I also tell her I think I'm staying at Keanu Reeves's house, which she totally doesn't believe. So, I go back to the third floor, snap some pictures and send them to her. She squeals because she's actually a huge fan.

"He's supposed to be dating Jamie Clayton. The two of them could have had sex in that very bed?"

Hmm. I hadn't thought of that. Nor do I know who Jamie Clayton is, but I'll let that go. But I know that Keanu Reeves was supposed to have dated Charlize Theron years ago. The thought she could have been naked and moaning on that bed has me all sorts of worked up.

I tell D I'll talk to her tomorrow and hang up. I unzip my pants and . . .

Something bangs against the front door. The chain rattles.

I freeze, zip up, and go to the top of the stairs. The door bangs open again and the chain rattles even louder. It stops.

My heart is racing. I dial 911. The phone is ringing

when I hear someone say my name.

CHAPTER NINETEEN

"Clive? Open the door!"

Aaaaaaaand I'm idiot. I hang up and race to the front door. I put the chain in place, effectively locking Gabriel out.

The front door is open enough for me to look out at him. "Dude, you look horrible," I say. "Coyle said you wouldn't be back for hours."

I close the door so I can unchain it and reopen it. "I mean, seriously, you look like you need a hug."

As he walks past me into the condo, Gabriel smiles but it doesn't reach his eyes. He takes off his jacket and throws it on the ground. Before I know what's happening, he's got his arms around me, hugging me. I feel super uncomfortable because I barely know the guy. But I don't want to pull away because I can tell he's crying.

He inhales sharply and walks away.

"Wait." I grab his arm. "What happened?"

He hangs his head. "They found another body."

I can't feel my legs. I'm terrified. Shocked. "Oh my god. Was it . . ."

He shakes his head. "They wouldn't tell me. Coyle had someone bring me here. They're watching the exits. He says it's to make sure no one gets in. But I think it's also to make sure we don't leave."

I pull Gabriel into another hug. "Damn. I'm so sorry."

We walk to the kitchen. Gabriel opens a cupboard over the sink and grabs two shot glasses. He pulls a bottle of tequila from a cupboard under the island. He tries to pour shots for us, but his hands are shaking. I grab the bottle from him, pour two shots and hand him one. After he downs it, he wipes tears from his eyes with the back of his hand and tells me what happened.

"Amy didn't answer her phone," he says. "Which is weird. You know Amy. She lives on her damn phone. I went up to her apartment. I knocked on the door, but there was no answer. I was about to head down to security, to see if they could buzz her or something, when Coyle and his partner Demena showed up. I noticed that Demena had a hand on the holster of her weapon and put my hands up. I stepped away from the door, and they asked me what I was doing there. So, I told them.

"Demena knocked on Amy's door. When she didn't get a response, Coyle tried the doorknob. It wasn't locked. As soon as we stepped inside, I knew something was very wrong. The furniture was turned up, cushions sliced open. It was significantly worse than how your apartment had been trashed. So, they started asking questions."

"And you decided not to be an idiot and told the truth."

Gabriel shrugs. "More or less. Demena took me downstairs to be questioned, while Coyle knocked on the neighbors' doors, looking for some sort of clue. It might have been faster if I reached out to my contacts and–"

"You have contacts?"

Gabriel shrugs. "It's . . . complicated. And using them has consequences. So, I sucked it up and went with Demena."

"What do you think happened to Amy?"

"One of two things." Gabriel runs his fingers through his sweat-damp hair. "Either she's fled the country and made it look like an abduction, or . . ." His voice trails away. He looks at the floor.

He doesn't want to say it. So, I do. "She's been abducted.

He nods. "That place was wrecked. Looked to me like someone was searching for something. Whatever it was, I don't think they found it. Which is probably good for Amy. Means there's a shot she's still alive." He sighs and wipes his eyes. "Coyle told me they'll have Amy's picture all over the news. They'll say she's a person of interested in the murder cases. Hopefully, someone will recognize her and know where she's been."

"Did they say anything about looking into the victims' families?"

Gabriel shook his head. "Not really. Even if they take the idea seriously, it will be several hours and lots of phone calls to verify the parents' work history. Which means we're done for tonight."

Gabriel excuses himself and heads for bed. Me, I'm too wired for sleep now, so I call Delilah again. I tell her Amy's missing and the police have found another body, one that might be Amy's.

"Whoa," she says. "Looks like you were right after all. How did you guess the connection?"

"It wasn't really guessing," I say. "Just logic. But what I don't get, the part that doesn't make any sense, is what happened to Jerry Tran? Odds are good he's the man in that video, but how does he connect with China? Did he work there, too? Shitty we don't have a way to find out more about him or Monica."

Delilah inhales softly, almost a pained sound. But she says nothing.

"What's up?" I ask.

"Well, I may actually have an in, a way to find out more information on Jerry Tran. But you probably won't like it."

"As long as it doesn't involve a Ouija board, I'm interested."

"Remember that guy I was on a date with last week? Well, his name is Trevor and he just so happens to work in the same law firm Jerry Tran did. That's how we met. In the building. Trevor just made junior partner. I'm sure he knows something about Jerry Tran. I can ask him."

Now that she's opening up, she's talking very fast, like she wants to get it all out. And she's right. I don't like it. Her voice perks up each time she says his name. And I'm completely and irrationally jealous. But I know I'm being stupid, so I say what a non-crazy person would say.

"Sure. Good idea." I spend the next ten minutes pretending I'm not jealous and trying to convince her I don't feel threatened. She tells me she'll call him right now and make a lunch date. She's done work at four tomorrow and says she'll call me after and tell me all about it.

"Can we meet up?" I ask. I suddenly miss her tons, and I'm sure it was nothing to do with her chatting up that stupidly handsome guy who's probably super rich. So, we make plans to have dinner together at the food court at the Eaton Centre.

Now, if you've never been to the Eaton Centre before, that might sound lame. But trust me, this is no regular food court. They have some of the best food in the city and hands down the best burger available. Knowing I'm going to see Delilah tomorrow makes everything a little bit better.

The good feeling doesn't last, though. I can't really call Amy a friend, but I've known her for years. And now she may be dead. Or she may be working with a serial killer who's trying to kill me. I'm not sure which option is worse.

***

I wake in the morning to an empty house. Gabriel left a note for me on the kitchen counter saying he was heading downtown to see Coyle, to try to find out if the body they found was Amy's. I search a few news sites on my phone and read up on the body that was discovered. No names have been released yet because the next of kin haven't been notified.

I didn't tell Gabriel I was planning on leaving, so of course he hasn't left me a spare key or anything. I feel completely stuck. As the day goes on and he doesn't show back up, I feel even more like a prisoner. I try to jerk off a few times, but I'm just not feeling it. What I really want to do is head up to Keanu Reeves's bedroom, but I definitely don't want Gabriel walking in on me doing that. So, instead, I watch a few episodes of Dexter on Netflix and take a nap.

By three in the afternoon, I realize Gabriel isn't coming back any time soon. If I want to make my date with Delilah, I'm going to have to leave the house without a key. I also don't have Gabriel's cell number or remember his last name. Which means I might not be able get back into the apartment. But, worst case scenario, I can get Coyle to call Gabriel. Or I can go back to Delilah's place and have wild crazy sex. That makes leaving the apartment easier.

Turns out I actually do know where I am. I didn't recognize the view from that high up, but I'm near Charles Street West and Bay Street. The Eaton Centre is only about a twenty-minute walk from here. At least it would be on a normal day. Today, the snow is heavy and most of the sidewalks haven't been plowed yet. Normally, I'd just take the subway, but I'm not meeting Delilah for a couple of hours. I have nothing but time. So I walk.

And as I walk, I think.

I start wondering why my father hasn't reached out to me. I mean, sure he's an inconsiderate jerk, but my name has been all over the news for days. My best friend has been murdered. Shouldn't that at least warrant a quick phone call?

I walk down Bay and find a Starbucks. I step inside to get out of the cold and to make a phone call.

I order a caramel macchiato and call my mom.

"Oh," I say. "Sorry. I didn't expect you to pick up. Aren't you at work?"

"Yes," she says. "But I saw your name and . . . Is everything okay, honey?"

"Fine. It's just, I was thinking. Has Dad reached out to you?"

She hesitates for a moment and I have my answer.

"Why didn't you tell me?" I ask.

She sighs. "I thought dealing with him after all this time was the last thing you needed. This was before you were asking about him, so I didn't think it was important."

"Where is he, Mom. Did Dad tell you were he is?"

She hesitates again. This time I wait for her to answer.

"He's in Mississauga," she says.

"Since when?" The last time I'd heard anything about my father, he was working in management for some company in Greece.

"For a few months."

"A few . . ." I stop. My voice is super loud. I only realize it because everyone in Starbucks is staring at me. I lower my voice to continue. "Don't you think the timing of his return is a tad suspicious? We have to tell the police."

"I've already told Detective Coyle," she says. "And he's already spoken with your father. He was one of the first people they spoke to after Kevin was found, specifically because the timing was so suspicious. I know I should have told you. I guess I was hoping you wouldn't find out."

"But why is he back? What is he doing here?"

I hear other voices murmuring on my mom's side of the call.

"I can't talk now," she says. "I have to get back to work. I promise I'll call you this evening and tell you everything. Okay? Are you somewhere safe?"

I look around. Everyone at Starbucks has gone back to ignoring me.

"Yes. I'm fine. I'll talk to you later."

Hanging up is the last thing I want to do, but I know she's right. That talk can wait. Instead, I try Googling my father but, just like Lucius Vitalli, there is next to nothing about my father online. Not because he's a secret guy. He just hates technology. And he's old.

I finish my drink and head back into the storm. All the way to meet Delilah, my head is inventing a million different reasons why my father is back in town. Not one of them is for anything good.

CHAPTER TWENTY

After I get to the Eaton Centre, I head directly to Chapters. It's the easiest place to waste time. I head to the top floor and browse the science fiction and fantasy section. I end up finding a new novel by Brandon Sanderson and settle down in a corner to read. No one disturbs me. After an hour and half, I buy the book and head to the food court.

I'm still a bit early, so I find a seat and send Delilah a picture of where I'm sitting. The place seats hundreds and it's already crowded. I open my browser and search for more information on Guangzho. Aside from tourist spots and reports on earthquakes, I can't find anything worth noting.

I spend some more time browsing Shinonach's website, but for such a large company it's got a really crap site. It is, however, a publicly traded company and has made tons of financial statements available online. I have no clue how to read a financial statement. I've no idea if the company is doing well or not. But as I skim through several quarterly reports, I notice something. Over the last year, a new line item has appeared on their income statement – extraordinary loss. It's listed at over three hundred million dollars and has an asterisk beside it. It takes me a while to skim through the PDF file to find out what that asterisk relates to. And then I see it: Reconstruction cost of Shunni Microsystems Holding Corporation after fire destroyed the production line.

I'm guessing that means Shinonach is more of an umbrella corporation and Shunni was one of its subsidiaries. I Google Shunni and fire. Bingo.

I see several articles from September of last year about a massive fire in a warehouse run by Shunni. Over two hundred workers died. None of the articles gives conclusive details on what caused the fire. However, several of them stated the fire was likely intentionally set by someone. This leads to other articles about deplorable working conditions at the factories and a string of suicides. Twenty-four Shunni employees had killed themselves at work within the last year.

I search for more recent articles and find one that claims to know how the fire started. A forty-five-year-old woman named Hu Li covered herself with flammable liquids and set herself on fire after a manager accused her of not working quickly enough. After the fire, Hu's family led protests in front of the factory for several days.

I put my phone away. I've learned a few things about Shinonach, but none of this information helps me get any closer to finding the killer.

I look around the food court and my eyes land on Delilah. She's unbuttoning her coat as she walks towards me. I stand up, smiling like an idiot.

She comes to me and we embrace. I kiss her lightly on the lips and we sit.

She puts her purse on the table and for the first time I notice how girly it is. Bright red with slender straps.

"That looks elegant," I say. Immediately, I wish I could take it back. I've never been the type to notice women's shoes or purses. But it makes Delilah smile.

"It's Coach."

She says that like I'm supposed to know what that means. Since I don't, I just nod and smile.

"Do you want to get food before we get caught up?" she asks.

My stomach answers for me. She heads to Liberty Noodle and I hit the Indian place whose name I never remember. We meet back at the table in fifteen minutes. I have enough food for three people. It barely fits on the table. But instead of calling me a pig, Delilah reaches over and helps herself to a piece of my naan.

"So, did you find out anything from the hunky lawyer?" My voice is a tad more bitter than I intended.

Delilah lowers her eyes at me and speaks slowly. "His name is Trevor. And yes. I found out quite a bit about Jerry Tran." She picks up chop sticks and starts eating her stir-fry. "Jerry had been with the company for over fifteen years. Everyone loved him, and they were crushed when he died.

He was found in the boardroom with his pants down. Trevor wasn't there when the body was found but he heard from someone who was. Word is Jerry totally killed himself, but it looked like an accident. Strangled by a neck tie. One end wrapped secured to a door, the other his throat."

I nod. So, the rumors were true. I've heard of this. Autoerotic asphyxiation. Jerking off as you cut off your air supply is supposed to heighten the orgasm. I like a good orgasm as much as the next guy, so I've looked into it. But any Google search you do will reveal how stupid that is. People die from it all the time. That's just silly. My thrills might get me arrested but not dead.

"So maybe he isn't related to all of this after all," I say. Still, something about this is nagging at me. "Did you find out what kind of work Jerry Tran did? Anything involving China or manufacturing?"

She shakes her head and sips her Coke. "Not even close. He was a copyright and patent lawyer His most recent client was some company in Mississauga."

Fuck.

Delilah reaches out and touches my hand. "What? You look like you're going to have a coronary."

I shake my head. "No. I'm fine. But I learned a few hours ago my father is at a new company in Mississauga."

"Along with 700,000 other people. This probably has nothing to do with him."

I sigh and play with my food. Suddenly I've lost my appetite. "You may be right. I'll have to let Coyle know about this. He can investigate."

Delilah frowns. "You really think all of this is about your father? You think he did something, and now someone is out to take revenge on him through you?"

"Either that or my father is involved in another way." I close my eyes to stop the room from spinning. I really want some valerian root right now. "I'll be right back."

I push up from the table. Delilah says nothing, just takes another piece of my naan and smiles.

Since I don't have valerian root with me, I head to the washroom to splash some cold water on my face.

The washroom is packed and anything but relaxing. Still, I head straight to the sinks and turn on a tap. The lights flicker. For a second it almost looks like a pair of eyes is looking back at me from inside the mirror. Red eyes. I blink repeatedly. The eyes keep staring at me.

The lights stop flickering. I must be very tired. I'm starting to see things. Which is bad. That hasn't happened since that time my mom had to have me committed. It would always happen in the dark. Something would trigger my memories of the basement when Banner had me on so many drugs it looked like the shadows were moving.

I enter a stall and lock the door. I lean my head against the cool metal of the door and take deep breaths until I get my head back together. Maybe it is time to get back on the meds, after all.

I hear creepy whispers coming from the stall next to me. I'm not sure if it's part of my delusion or if I'm really hearing it. The whispers say my name. And I recognize the voice.

"Poor little Clive," the voice says. "Want to make a video?"

I freeze. It's the man from the videos.

His words are light and musical, a taunt. Part of me screams to open the door, to run as far away as possible. Another part, much smaller, says I should open the door and confront him, see what he looks like. Before I can do either of them, I hear his stall door open. He's tall. I catch sight of the top of his head as he walks by. Short, strawberry blond hair.

And I don't need to see him now. I know who he is. The guy from the subway, the one I thought looked familiar.

And now the part of me screaming to confront him grows stronger. What is he going to do? We're in a very public place, surrounded by hundreds of people and security guards. I throw open the door and race out of the bathroom. But it's too late. I scan the crowds. There's no sign of him.

I've said before, I've learned to trust my instinct. Back when I was a kid, something told me Banner was a monster. But I didn't listen. My rational mind convinced me that monsters don't exist. But logic is wrong. I've always known monsters are real.

Just like I know, right in that moment, that Delilah is in trouble.

I run. I push through the crowd, pushing people aside as I run back to the table. I scream Delilah's name, vaguely aware that people all over the food court are stopping to stare at me. I don't care. All my attention is on the table. I see our food.

But Delilah is gone.

I scream, frustrated and powerless. Security guards are walking towards me. That's when I see her.

Amy.

She's standing on the stairs heading up to the next level, staring right at me. In her hands, I see a red purse. Delilah's purse.

I rush at her but don't get far. Three security guards rush me, pinning me to the ground. The harder I struggle to get free, the more I scream, the more they push me down.

There's nothing I can do. I'm just not strong enough to fight.

Amy gets away.

CHAPTER TWENTY-ONE

Hours pass. I'm back at the police station, sitting in the same spot I was in after Kevin's body was found. My head can't process thoughts. I've cried so much my eyes are on fire, and my body is all bruised from the security guards restraining me. As soon as the real cops showed up and found out who I was and what had happened to Delilah there was a whole bunch of apologies, but it doesn't matter.

The killer has Delilah. If we don't find her, he's going to kill her, just like he killed Kevin. And I wasn't strong enough or smart enough to stop it.

Coyle and his partner interviewed me for what felt like forever, but they're done now. They wanted me to call my mom, but I don't want her anywhere near me right now. Amy's seen her and that means she's in danger. But it's doubtful she knows where my mom lives. If she stays in Brantford, Mom should be safe.

Instead, I tell Coyle to call Gabriel. Turns out he didn't need to. Gabriel is still at the police station, being grilled by two cops I don't know. I get the feeling there's something else going on. Coyle looks nervous whenever he says Gabriel's name, which is kind of odd for a police officer.

I ask Coyle about the body that was found. I now know it wasn't Amy. He brushes me off and says it's classified, which sounds like such a bullshit answer. I mean, unless she was some sort of spy, how is her identify classified?

It's nearly ten at night when Gabriel is finally free. He stands by the exit and waves at me, but he doesn't come close to Coyle's office.

"What's going on?" I ask.

He shakes his head. "Not here. You okay?"

"Not even a little bit." I follow him through the nearly empty police station and out into the street. We don't say anything else until he opens the doors of his car and we're sitting inside.

"What did they tell you about me?" he asks.

"Um . . . nothing. Should they have?"

Gabriel starts the car. "No, they shouldn't have. The bloody idiots are going to blow my cover."

My head is throbbing. "Please don't tell me you're a spy or something. I've really had enough craziness today. I can't deal with delusions."

Gabriel smiles and pulls the car out onto the street. "Not a spy, Clive. But I'm not a stuntman, either. At least, not only a stuntman. Have you heard of CSIS?"

I turn slowly to look at him. I blink slowly. CSIS is the Canadian version of the CIA.

"You're freakin' kidding me. You are a spy."

Gabriel laughs. "Hardly. The closest I've ever gotten to a spy was reading files. I'm a librarian."

"Of course you are."

"It's a contract position. I spend twenty hours a week cataloguing committee reports and surveillance tapes. There's a full-time research position opening up in a few months, and I've got a good shot at getting it, as long as I keep my nose clean."

"So, I'm putting your job at jeopardy. Great."

He looks over at me. "You're not doing anything, Clive. This is all on Amy."

"Can't you call in your people to track her down?"

"Remember when I said keep my nose clean? Besides, we're not supposed to spy on our own citizens. We're not Americans. CSIS would only get involved if there was threat to national security. And honestly, I'd have no clue how to even tell them about this. I almost never deal with the actual security people. My superiors do that."

"They're not going to track me down and kill me because you've told me, are they?"

"Jesus, Clive. You watch too much TV. A few people know I work for CSIS. Amy was one of them. We were friends long before I started working there. She even helped me with my resume."

Gabriel is looking in his rear-view mirror a lot, like he's checking to make sure we're not being followed. Which makes me feel super paranoid. I look in the side mirror, but I can't see anything. Just a never-ending series of car lights behind us.

I slump into my seat. We ride in silence back to Keanu Reeve's place. When Gabriel stops the car, I don't get out immediately. Instead I ask a question.

"Whose body did they find?"

Gabriel grips the steering wheel. "It doesn't make sense."

I wait for him to continue, but he just stares out through the windshield.

"For fuck sake." I get out of the car and start walking towards to the elevator. I'm beyond tired. I hear Gabriel's door open, and I turn around. He's standing there by his car, and I want to scream at him, to hit him, to use him as a focus for all my frustration. He's the closest thing I have to a friend now that Kevin is dead, and Delilah is gone.

I shake my head. No. Delilah isn't gone yet. But I know a part of me is bracing for the worst. I'm already trying out the idea that Delilah is dead. Dead because of me.

And now I'm crying hysterically again. I sit down on the dirty floor of the underground parking garage. Gabriel walks over to me but says nothing. He sits down beside me and puts a hand on my shoulder. And waits.

When I get control of myself again, I push myself up to my feet. I give Gabriel my hand and help him up.

We don't say anything else as we walk to the elevator. I see two men standing by the elevator, one is a security guard, the other is a famous face.

I lean over to Gabriel. "Is that really Drake?"

He nods. "We've met. I can get you an autograph if you want."

I shake my head. I'm not really a fan, but it's still cool to see someone you've only see on TV before in person. It's like someone has been in your life for years but you've never really seen them, and then there they are . . .

I shriek.

Drake and the security guard look over me. Drake smiles, and I'm sure he thinks I've shrieked because I saw him. But that's not it.

I turn to Gabriel. "I know where I've seen the blond man before. I'm such a fucking idiot. He was there right in front of me the whole time."

I take out my phone and call Coyle. It only takes three rings for Coyle to pick up, but they feel like the longest three seconds ever. As soon as Coyle answers, I don't waste any time.

"You need to contact the owners of my apartment building," I say. My voice is surprisingly calm. "I finally remembered where I've seen that man before, the one with the strawberry blond hair. He's a security guard at my building."

CHAPTER TWENTY-TWO

After I hang up with Coyle I'm shaking, and I don't know if it's fear or excitement.

"Are you serious?" Gabriel asks. "You're sure he's one of our security guards?"

I nod and we're walking towards the elevator again. Drake and the security guard are gone, and I have this weird desire to write Drake a thank-you letter. If it wasn't for him, I don't know if I would have ever made the connection.

"Think about it," I say. "Most people never really see security guards. They only see the uniform. The security guard that was just here, what color hair did he have?"

Gabriel thinks for a moment. "I . . . I don't know. Blond? Maybe?" He shakes his head. "Damn. I can't remember anything about him except he had a slight tan."

"Exactly, I couldn't pick him out of a lineup to save my life. I've seen at least a few dozen people behind the security desk of our building. Most I've never even spoken to. I walk in the front door, and if they acknowledge my presence at all, it's a short nod."

I try to think back on the different security guards I've dealt with since I moved into the apartment. I remember the last time I saw the blond guy with the creepy voice, though.

It was the night I took Tonia home. He was the one that shushed us.

"Maybe it's a matter of selective perception," Gabriel says. "We look briefly, see the uniform, and our brain says the person isn't a threat. So we stop seeing them."

"I do that a lot. Focus on things that seem super important while blocking out other things." I shiver, thinking about the figure in my apartment. "That's how he got into my place. He had access to all the keys."

I wonder how many times he'd been in my bedroom. How many times had he watched me sleeping and I didn't know? Maybe that's how he recognized me from my videos. He could have been on my computer. He could know everything about me.

Gabriel pushes the button to call the elevator. "Take a breath, Clive. You're safe. Coyle and Demena have a frame of reference now, something to cross-reference. They'll look at the security video from the mall and cross-reference with the staff from the security agency. They'll have a name and address for the suspect within the hour."

I smile and nod, but I don't feel relieved. None of that will get Delilah back. I need to change the subject, focus on something else before that line of thought takes over again.

"So, are you going to tell me whose body they found or not?" I ask.

Gabriel hesitates for a moment and rubs his forehead. "I just don't know what it means. Maybe nothing. Amy and I used to go to this Korean barbeque place down on Queen Street. We were there all the time. And the body that was found, well, she worked there."

"She was Korean?"

"No. That's probably why she stood out. She was the only non-Asian working there."

"And you're sure her death is connected to this." I can't tell if I'm missing something or if Gabriel is purposefully leaving something else out. "Did she have a family member who worked in Guangzho? Or do you think Amy killed her for giving bad service?"

Gabriel gives me this look like he wants to hit me.

"Too soon?" I ask. "Look, I know she's your friend, but Amy is tied up with the murder of at least six people. Maybe seven." Another thought occurs to me. "Wait, you said this Korean place was on Queen, right? Where on Queen?"

"Two-hundred block of Queen Street West. Why?"

"Not sure." I scratch my head and walk towards the kitchen. I definitely need a beer. Gabriel follows, and I pass him one too. As we drink in silence, I start thinking of the things that don't make sense.

"Here's what we know. Someone appears to be taking revenge on westerners who worked at a factory in Guangzho at the time of an industrial accident. Not all the victims have ties to that factory, but enough do that it's unlikely to be a coincidence. They also take out Kevin's boss, a lawyer at the firm trying to hush up the accident. And when Kevin finds out about the event, they kill him too. But that doesn't make sense, does it? If they're angry about the event, wouldn't they want more people to know about it? Why aren't they making a statement, telling the whole world why they're killing?"

"Maybe because they're not James Bond villains who want to be caught." Gabriel leans against the fridge. "Establishing motive is the key element in proving guilt. Maybe they don't want to be found."

"Or maybe," I say, "maybe this isn't really about revenge. Maybe it's all about misdirection."

"You think Amy and this security guard want us to what . . . just think it's about China? Then why bother with the sex tape thing?"

I blush.

Gabriel holds up his hands in surrender. "You're the one who brought it up."

I sigh. "Yeah. I'm guessing Coyle didn't tell you that part." When Gabriel shakes his head, I make a decision to tell the truth. Kind of. "Without getting into details, let's just say I may have a few sex videos online and . . ."

"A few?" Gabriel's eyes raise. "What are you, a porn star?"

Wanting to die now. "No. Not even a little bit. But I maybe have done a few things and the security guard commented on the videos."

"Why?" Gabriel empties his drink and puts the bottle down. "For what purpose? If he's smart enough to do all this and not get caught, why risk reaching out to you? Why not just kill you and be done with it?"

I stare at him. "You know, you really suck at the whole making-me-feel-safe thing. But I get your point. He's taunting me. Repeatedly. Almost like all of this is just for me." And it hits me. I feel the heat rush from my body, and I desperately want to sit down.

Gabriel is beside me. I feel him help me over to the couch, but I'm only vaguely aware of moving.

"What's going on in there?" he asks.

I inhale slowly. "It's not all about me. All of this, all these deaths are aimed at my father. They want me scared, they want me all over the news to punish him. Maybe they're blackmailing him, forcing him to do something or they'll kill me too. But that doesn't feel right. I think whatever happened in Guangzho is mostly my father's fault. He killed all those people and because of that, my best friend is dead."

Gabriel is quiet for a moment, his eyes darting from place to place as if he's searching his mind. "I don't know, Clive. Maybe. But what does that have to do with the girl from the restaurant? Or Jerry Tran and Monica?"

I shake my head. "Say, what was the woman's name, the one who worked in the restaurant?"

"Melissa. Her name was Melissa MacDougall."

My jaw drops. "Are you fucking serious?" I take out my phone and search for one of the pictures Kevin sent me. "You mean this Melissa?"

Gabriel stares at the picture, his eyes wide. "Do I even want to know how you got that?"

I turn the phone off. "Kevin sent it to me. At least I thought it was Kevin. They hooked up, but he told me he hadn't seen her for awhile. What if these pictures weren't actually taken by Kevin? What if they were taken by the security guard as another way to taunt me?"

"But why? How does this hurt your father?"

I lean my head back against the couch. "Shit if I know. Maybe the problem is we're looking for logic from a psychopath. Sometimes evil people do evil things for reasons we can't understand."

Gabriel leans his head back too. "True dat. You should see some of the crazy person logic I get researching terrorist cells. They think they have the whole world figured out, but they're seeing things through this really distorted lens. There's this eco-terrorist group in British Columbia that believes oil pipelines are doing something to destroy nature. So what do they do? Blow up the pipelines, causing massive oil spills that destroy nature."

"Psychos. When I was younger, something happened to me. A guy took me and . . ."

"Jesus."

I shrug. "It was brutal. I can't believe I'm actually sharing this. I never really talk about it. Maybe it's the whole almost being killed again thing." In my mind I'm back in the basement. "His name was Zacharia Banner and he took a whole bunch of kids. I was too scared to talk but one kid wasn't. Todd Michaluk. He asked Banner why he was doing this, why he took us, why he . . . hurt us. The first few times, Banner just laughed and kept on having his fun. But the last time Todd asked, Banner said the shadows told him to do it. Then he cut out Todd's tongue."

Gabriel squirms in his seat.

"He used to stare into the darkness and whisper. Made my skin crawl. He even had names for the creatures in the shadows. Carla and Sanchez. How fucked up is that?"

Gabriel is trembling now. He can't even look at me.

"The thing is, I was so fucked up on sleep deprivation, pain and whatever drugs he was feeding us to keep us pliable, sometimes I saw them too. Glowing red eyes in the shadows."

"My god," Gabriel jumps off the couch and starts pacing. "This is so fucked up. It can't be a coincidence. Can it? What are the odds? Look, Clive, this may be hard to believe, but maybe you weren't seeing things. Maybe the things in the shadows are real."

"Fuck off."

"No, I'm serious." He's chews on his thumbnail, which is never a good sign. I do that sometimes too when my delusions are getting too strong. "There are things in the world you don't know about. I've seen hints of them doing research for CSIS. Reports from all over the world. Things moving in shadows, making people do things. There was even this village in Africa wiped out by shadow people. I know it sounds crazy, but I read the reports. Tell me, did the guy, Banner, did he ever use the word—"

My phone rings.

I've never been more happy to hear a ring tone. Gabriel is moving into full-on psychotic delusion here. So I answer the phone, smiling.

"Hello, Clive," the voice says.

I nearly pee my pants. It's the sing-song happy voice of the security guard.

"Where is she?" I ask. I'm gripping the phone so tight I feel like I might break it. So, I force myself to take a breath. "What have you done with Delilah?"

"Not as much as I'm going to. Tell me, Clive, have you checked Facebook recently?"

The room starts to swim. I know I have to check Facebook, but I also know I don't want to see Delilah's dead body. Not like Kevin. I can't bear to live through that again.

"She's not dead yet," the security guard says. "But she will be soon. You know, he said you would be smarter. I thought you'd already know where we'd taken her. Guess he was wrong about you."

"He who?" I ask. Is he talking about my father? Was I wrong? Maybe all of this wasn't to target my father. Maybe he's been involved all along.

"I'm not telling."

I can hear Amy laughing in the background.

"Check Facebook now, Clive, before I take the picture down." The security guard's voice grows chilling and steely. "Move quick, asshole, or she's dead. You have one hour."

Then the call is over.

I look up. Gabriel isn't there. He's in the kitchen talking on his phone. I hear Coyle's name and realize he's calling the police but wanted to do it far enough way that the security guard wouldn't hear him.

"I can do this," I say. I open up the Facebook app and find Delilah's wall. I think I'm prepared for it and maybe I am. I manage not to scream.

Delilah is naked, bound to a chair under a single bare incandescent bulb. I select the photo to make it full screen and click on the three dots in the upper right corner to bring up the save photo option. I open my email app and forward the image to Coyle.

"Coyle's on his way," Gabriel says. "He says not to move."

I know not moving is the smart thing. But I also know I'm beyond that now. As soon as I saw the picture, I knew where they are keeping her. If traffic is good, it will take forty-five minutes to get there. If not, we'll be too late.

I jump off the couch, run to Gabriel and grab his phone. "Coyle, it's not going to happen. I refuse to sit by and watch as someone else dies. Arrest me later for obstruction if you want. For now, whatever you do, don't come here. Send units to Gateway Industrial Park in Mississauga."

"What? Why there?"

"That's where they're holding Delilah," I say.

"And you know this how?"

"Because he sent me a picture." I say the hard part. "And that's where my father works. At the local headquarters of Shinonach."

CHAPTER TWENTY-THREE

"I'll drive." Gabriel is putting on his coat and he has his keys in his hands. "But you need to calm down first. You're not going to do anyone any good like this. Go throw some water on your face."

"We don't have time." I have my hand on the doorknob.

"Exactly. So don't argue. The police will have cars at the warehouse long before we get there. For all you know, they'll already have Delilah rescued by then."

Or she may be dead.

Gabriel slaps me. Hard.

"Hey!" I hate him but, what do you know, it actually did work. It stopped my head from spinning. I also hate that he's giving me this sly little look like he knew it was going to work. "Fine. I'll go splash water on my fucking face. Happy?"

"Ecstatic."

I walk to the bathroom, but water isn't going to be enough to calm me down. Gabriel was right about one thing. If I'm all hyped up on fear, I might miss something again. I can't afford to miss anything else. The local Shinonach headquarters is the first place we should have looked for

Delilah, but I let my emotions muddle my brain. Also, my head is obsessing over something the security guard mentioned.

He said you would be smarter.

Who said that and why? What if this is all some sort of test? He made it sound almost like an initiation.

But I can't think about that now. So, instead of hitting the bathroom, I get four valerian root pills when I get to my room. I have nothing to take them with, so I put them in my pocket and walk to the kitchen for a glass.

That's when I hear it.

A loud, solid thud.

I almost call out to Gabriel but my fight/flight alarm bell screams, telling me to run, to hide. I start second-guessing myself. There are tons of reasonable explanations for that sound.

I hold my breath and listen. The only thing I hear is the beating of my heart and the whir of the central air system pumping heat through the rooms.

If Gabriel dropped something, he would have called out, said something. Which means . . .

My heart beats faster now. My mind traces the layout of the condo. Only one exit unless I want to rappel off the balcony with mountain climbing equipment. Which I don't have.

So, I do the smart thing. I step back into the bedroom, lock the door, and pull out my phone.

Nothing.

I have no signal at all.

What the fuck? Immediately my mind goes into overdrive. The killer is here. They've knocked out Gabriel and are using something to jam cell phone signals to stop me from calling the police. Logic brain is telling me I'm jumping to conclusions, but I don't listen to that. I know I'm right.

I put the phone in my pocket and unlock the door. Hiding isn't an option now. The killer must know where I am. What's really screwing me up is realizing he was probably already in the apartment when he called me, hiding in a closet or maybe up on the third floor. It's just like that old horror movie, When a Stranger Calls. He wanted me to call the police, to send them far away to save Delilah. As soon as I did that, I was vulnerable.

No one would think to come for me now.

And if Gabriel was knocked out, it was time for me to save myself.

Time to man up.

Maybe for once, my father is right.

I open the door.

I look down the hall. Nothing moves. No sounds. I know I need a weapon and think of going to the kitchen. But they would expect that. They? Hmm. I guess that makes sense. Maybe it's not just the serial killer. Amy could be with him, too. So, instead, I go to Gabriel's room and hope he doesn't have what I'm looking for on him.

Gabriel might be dead. I push that thought away. No time to worry about that now. If he is, there's nothing I can do to help him. If he's still alive, I'm his only hope.

I slip into Gabriel's room and lock the door. The lights are off, and I don't want to give away my position, so I use the flashlight on my phone to search through his luggage.

Heavy footsteps walk down the hall. I hear something scraping. My mind gives me a clear picture of the serial killer. He's walking towards me, dragging a knife along the wall.

It's not in his luggage, so I start going through Gabriel's clothing. I thought gay guys were supposed to be neat or something. Gabriel's a worse slob than me. He's got jeans and dirty socks lying everywhere. But it's not in the jeans either.

I hear the click of a door opening and my heart skips. My mouth is dry, and for a second I forget to breathe. He must have opened to door to my room. Which means I'm running out of time.

There's a chest of drawers opposite the bed. I open it as quietly as possible, moving clothes out of the way. And there it is.

I pick up the metal rod I'd seen Gabriel use before, the thing he called an asp. The handle is only a little longer than my hand and is covered in vinyl. Gripping it, I feel immediately less vulnerable. There are no buttons, so it takes me a second to figure out how to open it. I think back to how Gabriel did it. I flick my wrist and it extends to a baton nearly as long as my arm.

The doorknob jiggles.

Out of time.

Gabriel's room, like mine, has an ensuite bathroom. I rush to it, flip on the light and lock the door, shutting it immediately. But not from the inside, I'm hoping this tricks the killer. You can see the light is on through the small opening at the bottom of the door. The plan is that he'll rush in here, see the light and believe I'm inside. While he's busy breaking down that door, I'll have time to strike.

I hope.

The doorknob jiggles again and I wait for it to smash open. I'm lying on my stomach behind the bed, the extended baton still in my hands. If he checks here first, I'm done for. My position is completely vulnerable.

The door smashes open. I hear it bounce off the wall.

Silence.

I take shallow breaths, staying as quiet as possible. Can't make any sound.

I hear the scraping sound again. And footsteps. They walk into the room slowly and stop in front of the bathroom. From where I lie, I can't see him. But I can smell him. He's wearing a musky cologne.

He turns the bathroom doorknob and, finding it locked, laughs.

"Time to stop running, Clive," he says in that soft, musical voice. "Time to play."

I hear something slam into the bathroom door. That's my cue. I push myself to my feet and rush at him. He turns to face me, and I see he's got something in his hand — a knife. I swing the extended baton at his hand and hear bone crack. The killer howls in pain and drops to his knees. Before he can recover, I swing again, smashing the baton towards his head. His eyes roll back, and he crumples. I'm not sure if I killed him or even knocked him out, but I'm not going to wait to find out.

I need to find Gabriel. I run out of the room and hear crackling sounds. I look down to see wires sticking out of my chest. I'm flailing. Every nerve in my body screams in pain. I collapse in a puddle, twitching.

I'd forgotten about Amy.

***

I don't exactly pass out, but it's some time before I can move again. By then, it's too late. Amy secures my hands and feet with those thick plastic ties used for securing cables and pipes. They're just like the ones Banner used. She sticks something in my mouth, so I can't scream. Leaving me on the floor, she goes to check on the guy I hit with the asp. I hear murmuring voices and there goes all my hope. I'd assumed the blow to the head would have killed him. Guess I didn't hit him as hard as I thought. I hear his footsteps come out of the bedroom and he kicks me in the gut.

"Not yet," Amy says. "He has to be alive for the next part."

"Stupid mutt," the killer says, his accent suddenly stronger. "Broke my hand, ya did. But you're my arse monkey now."

He spits on me and kicks me again. He grabs the plastic tie that's binding my feet together and pulls me into the living room. My head bounces against the floor a few times so I lift it up. There's a wooden chair placed in front of the window. Gabriel is tied to a similar chair at the far end of the room. His head's hanging down and he's not moving. From here, I can't tell if he's breathing.

The killer pushes me into the chair by the window. I know I should fight back. But my muscles still aren't responding properly.

"Make sure those bonds are tight," he says. "He's tougher than he looks."

"Of course he is," Amy said. "That's what we've been saying all along."

I really want to ask who this "we" is, but I can't speak.

Amy walks over to Gabriel and pushes his head back. I see blood dripping down from his scalp.

"We should have killed him," the killer says.

"Kill Gabriel?" She shakes her head. "Not while I'm here. Killing Clive is the last step. Then both of us move on."

And there you have it. She actually said they are going to kill me. I knew it, but to actually hear someone say they are going to kill you and be powerless to stop it . . .

I start crying.

The killer laughs. He kisses my eyes. I try to push away from him, but I have no leverage. My struggling makes him laugh more.

"Do you have the camera?" he asks.

"Right here." Amy reaches into a black duffle bag and retrieves a small video camera and a retractable tripod. She places the camera on the tripod and sets it down in front of me. She presses a button and a red light flashes on. She picks up something that looks like a black walkie-talkie. It's has an antenna and blue lights blink along the front. She presses a button on the side. There's a hissing sound and the blue lights fade.

That must be the thing blocking my cell phone signal. When I make a break for it, I'll have to remember to grab that on the way.

The killer walks over to the bag and takes out two things. The first is a Lillie doll. He uses his good hand to toss it to Amy. The second is a very large, very black metal knife.

I scream but the sound is pale and fragile.

The killer kneels before me and looks me in the eye. "I'm sure you're asking yourself why. That's what all the others asked me, right when they found themselves in exactly the same spot you are." He brings the knife to the bottom of my shirt and pulls up. It's incredibly sharp, slicing easily through the fabric. I turn away and he slices again, until my bare chest is exposed. "So, go on. Ask me."

I close my eyes and feel the tip of the knife against my chest.

"Open your eyes or I take a nipple."

I comply and look back at him, fully seeing him for the first time. With his ice-blue eyes and strawberry blond hair, he's very attractive. He looks to be the sort of person you immediately trust. Like a priest or a movie star.

Amy is beside me now, her hands running over my exposed skin. "Don't be silly, Paeder. You know he can't ask questions unless you remove the gag. Do you want to remove it?"

"In time." He takes the knife the to the hem of my right pant leg. And cuts. The knife slices through the jean material like butter. And I have a very clear idea of what that knife will do to my flesh.

Amy goes back to the bag and takes out a syringe. She fills the needle with a clear liquid. Banner injected me with something back when he took me. It nearly paralyzed me, stopped me from speaking. And it made me see things.

I try to throw myself out of the chair.

The killer, whose name I guess is Paeder, flicks the knife across my chest and draws blood.

"Stop. Moving." He takes the blade to the plastic tie binding my feet and slices through it. He rips the remnants of the jeans from my one leg and starts working on the next. "Stay quiet."

Or what? You'll kill me? If I don't so something they're going to torture, rape and kill me slowly. I'd rather die quickly than let that happen. There's no way I'm going to stop fighting. I just have to take my chance when it comes.

Amy sticks the needle in my arm and immediately I go slack. Only, I'm not as numb as I'm pretending to be. I don't have a clue what she gave me, but my arm feels warm now.

"Like a baby," Amy said as she pulls out my gag. I'm not an idiot so I don't scream. That would only result in getting the gag put back in and probably more of the drug stuck in me. Instead, I wait.

Paeder finishes slicing off the other leg of my jeans and pulls the fabric away. "Now you can ask me."

I forced myself to blink slowly, as if nearly asleep.

He puts the knife to my crotch. "I said ask."

So, I do. "Why are you doing this? Why me?"

He smiles. "Because I can." He slips the knife under the crotch of my jeans. I can feel the cold metal against my penis. "And because she chose you."

Paeder cuts away my underwear. He takes a slice and holds it in front of his nose, breathing in the stench. I want to vomit. He stands up, grabs the black duffle bag and leaves the room.

My brain is getting foggier now, like when I've taken too much valerian root. Thinking is more difficult, but I've learned to function this way. I'm not sure how long I have before the drug's effects overtake me. I need to get smart very quickly or I'm dead.

I've done my research on crazy people. Everything Paeder and Amy are doing right now is to scare me. They need me to be afraid. My best option is to look bored, to remove myself from the conversation. I need to make this all about them. Manipulators don't like to be manipulated. If you have a chance to escape, make them feel they have all the power. They'll get sloppy and you can run. That's not an option here, so I need to push them. If I turn the tables, maybe they'll make a mistake.

Or maybe they'll kill me. That could happen too.

"You doing okay, Amy?" I ask. "You're looking a little pale."

She frowns. "I'm fine. You're the one in trouble."

"You sure? You look like you have a fever."

She reaches for her purse and pulls out a compact. She checks her reflection quickly and shoves the mirror back in her purse. But not before fixing her hair.

I stare at her, trying to look right through her as if she isn't there. She blinks, startled.

"This is because of Shinonach?" I ask. "Because of my father? Did he and the others cause the accident? Is this some sort of revenge? Tell me, Amy, did you lose someone in the explosion? Did he hurt your feelings?"

Amy blinks again. Unexpectedly, she laughs. "Oh, Clive. So close but not quite close enough. We're not going to kill you because your father caused the accident. We're doing this because your father couldn't keep his big mouth shut. You see, he and the others leaked information about the incident that has resulted in a very messy lawsuit, one I'm doing a very good job of shutting down."

She smiles at the camera and uses the fingers of one hand to brush back the hair of the Lillie doll she holds in the other. She may talk tough now, but I've spotted a weakness. I need to keep pushing.

"So, this is about getting your uncle's approval?" I shake my head. The drug in my system is getting stronger but I can't let up now. "Let me guess. He doesn't take you seriously because you're just a dumb bitch with a doll fetish. Tell me, is it working? Have you murdered enough people for him to see you as an equal yet?" I force myself to yawn and look bored.

Amy clenches her fists and growls. "Shut up. Your death is a lesson. No one betrays the Council." Amy points at the camera. "I don't need my uncle's approval. I already have it. You want to know why we killed the others and why we're going to kill you?"

"Because it's fun," Paedar says.

Amy smiles. "Well, it is a little fun. But mostly it's a lesson." She points at the camera. "We're compiling a training tape we can show to new recruits. Remember your oaths, keep quiet, and don't fuck with us. Or we will fuck with your loved ones in ways you can't imagine."

She's getting angry, which is good. Angry people make mistakes.

"What the fuck is up with the dolls?" I ask. My vision is getting cloudy. I might not have much more time.

"Do you know who invented the Lillie doll?" Amy asks. "Lillie is one of the most successful lines of dolls ever released and most people think it was invented by a man, Matthew Kovel. He started the Denkov toy line with his business partner Elliott Denver. The Lillie doll was their first big hit. Only, the part of the story no one talks about is that Lillie wasn't Matthew's idea. It was his wife's. Ida Kovel came up with the revolutionary idea of realistic children's dolls. It was her idea to use Saturday morning cartoons to heavily advertise them. She's the one that made her entire family rich, and the only thing she's remembered for is being married to some guy."

"So, you're supposed to be a feminist murderer?" I smile. "Like an equal opportunity nut job?"

Amy throws the doll at my face. It hits me just below the eye. Its feet scratch me, drawing blood.

I open my eyes in time to see Amy slap me.

"You condescending little fuck," she says. "Killing you isn't what makes me a feminist. This is about sending a message. To my uncle and the rest of the Council. I'm sick and tired of being an afterthought. My uncle put us in this position by trusting the wrong people. People like your father. I'm the one getting us out of it."

She's close now. I can make my move.

Paeder walks back in the room and I scream.

He's wearing that creepy living doll costume, the one he had on in that video with Michael. Black latex covers every part of his body except his doll-like face. The suit enhances his hips and ass, making him look more feminine. The black latex glistens like it's covered in Vaseline and makes a strange swishing sound as he walks towards me. For a second, I wonder how he got dressed in that with one broken hand. My mind focuses on something more important – there's a crazy man dressed like a living sex doll coming towards me with a knife his hand.

I know I'm out of time. I need to do something quickly or he's going to bring out the metal spike. I can't live through that again. I can't.

So, I start laughing.

"Oh, dear God," I say. "That is pathetic." I know they need me to be afraid. I can't give them what they want, or I'll be dead. "Tell me, Peter, are you naked under there? Is that to hide the fact you have a small penis?"

Amy hits me again. "His name is Paeder, asshole. Paeder Ferris. You would do well to remember the name of the man who's going to kill you."

"Does he need to inflate himself first?"

Amy hits me again.

"Enough," Paeder's voice comes out of the creepy living doll. "If you can't control yourself, Amy, leave the room."

"You don't get to tell me what to do!" Amy inhales sharply and wipes sweat from her forehead. "I am going to enjoy watching you die, Clive Dufault. And as for Paeder's penis, I've seen it. It is very large. If you live long enough, maybe you'll see it too."

Paeder puts down the knife and picks up something else.

Two metal spikes.

"People with big penises don't need to overcompensate." My mouth is dry, but I force myself to spit. "You're pathetic. Both of you. Do whatever you want. I'm bored now."

Amy punches me again. My head flings back and hits the top of the chair. I see stars.

"Go," Paeder says. "We're going to have to edit this part of the tape out if you want the Council to take you seriously."

I focus all my attention on Amy. She's furious now, her face red and her lips trembling with rage. I blow her a kiss. She stomps out of camera shot. I look past her and see something else. Something that makes me very happy.

Gabriel's chair is empty.

I giggle. Trying to sound as condescending as possible, I look up at Paeder. "Oh dear. Did you lose something?"

Paeder looks over his shoulder. "Fuck. Amy, you said Gabriel was out. Find him quickly."

Amy races from the room.

Paeder turns back to me, his face directly in front of mine so close I can see my reflection in the pupils of his eyes.

And there it is. My chance.

I throw my head forward, smashing my forehead into the bridge of his nose. Or at least where I hope his nose is. The weird fake face makes it hard to be sure. Paeder stumbles, and I'm on my feet. Hands still tied, I push out with them, striking him in the chest. He tries to steady himself. But his costume is slippery and awkward. He falls to the ground.

I have about ten seconds to get out of my bonds before he recovers. Luckily, plastic ties are about the easiest thing in the world to get out of. If they'd used rope or police-grade ties, I'd be screwed. Like I said, these are the same type of restraints Banner used on me. I became obsessed with how to get out of them. I've watched dozens of videos on how to escape these ties. I've even practiced hundreds of times. What can I say? Once I put my mind to something, I do it.

I bring my hands to my face and use my teeth to tighten the ties as much as possible. I make sure the locking mechanism is in the space between my hands. Although it looks to be the strongest part of the restraints, it's actually the weakest. I bring my hands up overhead, bend over slightly, then using all my strength, swing my arms down using my whole body as a wedge.

The plastic snaps. My hands are free.

I pick up the chair and smash it down on Paeder. Several times. When he stops moving, I grab the cell phone jammer.

"What the hell?" It's Amy's voice.

I look up to see her running towards me, another taser in her hand. I throw the cell jammer at her and she ducks. I need to close the distance between us, or she's going to taser me, so I don't take the time to think. I just act. I charge at her, body-checking her to the ground. She falls, and I punch her repeatedly in the head. She tries to lift the hand with the taser in it, and I punch her in the wrist. Her hand goes numb and she screams in pain. I grab the taser and roll off her.

Before she can recover, I'm on my feet, and I point the weapon down at her. I don't give her a warning. I don't tell her to stay down.

I just shoot her. As the wires hit her, her body convulses.

I drop the weapon and the convulsions stop.

Part of me really wants to kill her. I don't mean a little part, I mean like every part of my body is screaming at me to kill her. But I don't. I'm not really sure why.

"I need to call the police," I say.

I remember that my cell should be in my pants. I go back to the chair and go through the pockets of my destroyed jeans to retrieve my phone. I dial 911. When it starts ringing, it's the most glorious sound I've ever heard.

I tell the woman working dispatch what's happened. She probably doesn't believe a word I'm saying because I sound surprisingly calm. But I tell her the address and mention Coyle's name and . . .

Something slams into me from behind.

The phone goes flying and my head slams to the floor.

Paeder in his latex costume stands there. He must have tackled me. He's only got one metal spike in his hands now, and I'm suddenly very aware of how naked I am.

"You know what I'd like," Paeder says. "I'd like to take you home to meet my family. My brother Sasha would have fun with you. But there's no time for that now. I'm going to stick these through your eye sockets. You'll bleed out long before the police get here."

The lights flicker. For a second, it sounds like the shadows are laughing at me. I remember this feeling. It must be the drug they injected me with. Causing auditory hallucinations. My legs get weak. Pretty soon I won't be able to stand.

I hear a click. A gun being cocked.

I look behind me and see Gabriel standing in the hallway. He's got a very large gun pointed directly at Paeder.

"Kill him," I say. "His kind always gets back up."

"I know." Gabriel pulls the trigger. Paeder's body jerks back. He looks down at a hole in his latex costume. He falls to his knees. He has his hands up, pleading.

Gabriel pulls the trigger again.

As Paeder collapses to the ground, Gabriel stumbles. He flicks the safety on this gun and places it on the floor even as he's falling. I slowly get to my feet and go to him.

"Gabe? Are you okay?" I push back the hair from his head. His head wound is still bleeding. That can't be good. But it also can't be good that the room is getting darker. I'm not sure if the lights are really going out or if it's just the drugs in my system. But it feels colder.

"Don't . . ." Gabriel says. "Don't call me Gabe. And stay out of the shadows. They're watching us."

"What are you talking about?" I look around. The lights are still flickering, but only a little.

Gabriel doesn't answer. His eyes close and he goes limp.

I put my fingers to his throat and try to check for a pulse, but honestly I have no clue what I'm doing. I put my arm around him and hold him up. I'm not sure if I'm safe yet but the police are on their way. And the bad guys aren't moving.

The part of me that wanted to kill Amy is screaming at me again. It's telling me to put a bullet in her brain, to go make sure Paeder is actually dead. For all I know, he could be wearing body armor under that latex suit. He could be faking everything, just waiting for me to slip up. My fight/flight instinct is screaming at me to lock myself in a bedroom. But I can't leave Gabriel out here, and I can't move him.

So, I wait.

The drugs make me pass out before the police arrive.

CHAPTER TWENTY-FOUR

I wake up staring at the ceiling, a bright light flashing in my eyes. For a moment, I don't react. I don't know who has me and I scream. I thrash about, trying to get to my feet.

"Easy, son," a voice says. My eyes turn to the speaker and focus on him. It's Coyle. He puts his flashlight in his pocket and helps me sit up. I'm still naked, but someone has thrown a blanket over my lower body.

"What did they give me?" I ask.

Coyle shakes his head. "We don't know but it's over. Amy is in custody now and Gabriel's awake."

"What about Paeder? Is he dead?"

Coyle looks away. "Gabriel mentioned he shot another suspect. But he wasn't here when we arrived."

I feel cold. "You have got to be kidding me!" I feel like punching something, but I barely have the strength to make a fist. "Gabriel shot him. Twice. I knew he should have shot him in the head. Why doesn't anyone ever shoot the bad guys in the head?"

"Head shots are hard to make," Coyle says. "And, despite what the movies have you believe, most people don't get up after being shot in the chest. We found a trail of blood leading to the stairwell. That confirms he's shot and bleeding out. Whoever this man is—"

"Paeder Ferris," I say. "Amy called him Paeder Ferris. He's about six foot two inches. Has strawberry blond hair and blue eyes." When I first saw Paeder up close, I thought he looked like a movie star. Now, I know which one. "He actually looks like a young Robert Redford."

Coyle takes out his notepad and writes something. "We know what he looks like, remember? We saw him on the videotapes. The security company who hired him says he's been working under the name Christopher St. Clair. We're working under the assumption that's a fake name. But we have his fingerprints and his picture. It's just a matter of time before we catch him."

I remember something else and feel like the worst human being ever. "Delilah. Is she . . .?"

Coyle puts a hand on my shoulder. "She's fine. We found her tied up in the warehouse, just like you said she would be. She didn't seem to be injured, but we're having her checked out at the hospital just to be safe. Both you and Gabriel will be going there next."

"I told you I'm fine."

I turn my head and see Gabriel sitting on a couch. Demena is beside him.

"Sure you are," Demena says. "But you're still going to the hospital."

I notice there are several other uniformed policemen in the condo. And just like that, it feels over. At least for the moment I feel safe again. Amy is in custody. It feels like the last ten minutes of a thriller. If Coyle was black, they would cast Morgan Freeman to play him in the Netflix film.

"Help me to the couch," I say.

Coyle hesitates for a moment, but only for a moment. He gives me his hands, helping me to my feet. I wrap the blanket around me and Coyle leads me over to sit beside Gabriel. As soon as I'm settled, he and his partner go to check the rest of the condo.

"Your friend is going to be super pissed," I say. "You got blood all over his apartment."

Gabriel winces. "He'll manage. He's a Buddhist."

I want to ask him if this really is Keanu Reeves's place, but that would require admitting I've been snooping. So I let it slide. Instead, I ask him about something else.

"What did you mean? Just before you passed out you said, 'The shadows are watching.' How exactly are the shadows watching?"

Gabriel looks over at the cops. "Forget I said anything. It was just the drugs."

"But before Paeder called, I was telling you about Banner, how I saw glowing red eyes in the shadows when he took me. And you said—"

"Forget what I said." Gabriel turns to me, really intense. He smiles as if nothing is wrong. "There's no such thing as creatures that live in the shadows, Clive. That's crazy talk."

Don't ask me how. Maybe it's because I'm good at recognizing patterns or maybe I've just come to know Gabriel. Either way, there is one thing I'm one hundred percent sure about.

Gabriel just told me a lie.

I stare at the floor and let the matter drop. But an idea is forming. As soon as this is all over, I need to pay a visit to someone. Someone I haven't seen in a very long time.

***

The rest of that week totally sucks. After days of being questioned by the police and being hounded by the media for statements, I go to my best friend's funeral. Kevin is buried in Brantford. It's a large event. Hundreds of people. They manage to keep the news crews outside the cemetery gates, but just barely.

I hug Kevin's mom. Hell, I even hug Jay the jerk.

The only thing that makes it slightly bearable is Delilah. She is there for me the whole time, holding my hand and telling me it's okay to cry. I tell her the same thing. She's different since the whole kidnapping thing. Although, in a way, I think we're even more perfect for each other than before. She can completely understand me now . . . which makes me incredibly sad. No one should ever really know how it feels to be like this. So completely vulnerable all the time because you know, at any moment, someone crazy could step into your life and fuck you up.

Gabriel and I went back to our old apartments. I say hi to him when I see him, but he doesn't want to talk much. But today, the day of the funeral, I decide he doesn't get a choice in that.

Before heading to the funeral, I knocked on his door. After a while he opens it, but I can tell he doesn't really want to talk to me.

"You're a fucking idiot," I say.

He takes a step back.

I put my hand on the door so he can't shut it in my face. "So, here's the thing. You're my friend now, and I'm not going to let you pull away because you feel guilty or some shit."

"I don't feel guilty."

"Whatever. You haven't said three words to me since Coyle took us to the hospital. And I won't have it. In a few hours I'm heading to a cemetery to bury my best friend. You and Delilah are now my only friends in the whole world. So, stop being a jerk and just be my friend. Deal?"

I hold out my hand.

Gabriel looks at it for a long time, like I'm holding a weapon on him or something. Finally, he shakes it. He grabs his coat, puts on his shoes, and steps out into the hallway.

"Where are you going?" I ask.

"To the funeral. Obviously." He sets his alarm, locks the door behind him, and puts his arm around my shoulder. "Most people would have a hard time recovering from what you just went through. You are a lot stronger than you look, Clive Dufault."

"Yeah," I say. "A lot of people tell me that."

I still don't know what Paeder meant when he said, He said you'd be smarter. But I'm going to find out.

As soon as the funeral's over, I kiss Delilah and tell her I'll call her later tonight.

She gives me this strange look, like I've started speaking German or something.

"I need to talk to someone, someone from my past. And I don't want you anywhere even close to him. Gabriel will drive me there."

"Does Gabriel know this yet?" Delilah asks.

I shake my head. "Nope. But he owes me. And since he won't tell me the truth, there's only one other person I can ask."

As Delilah walks away, I have a rush of emotion. I love her. I want to trust her. But this question keeps gnawing at me.

Why did they let her live?

Amy and Paeder never let anyone else survive. They could have just as easily taken a picture of Delilah while she was alive to use as bait and killed her so she couldn't talk. Not that I want her to be dead, of course. But something about this bugs the crap out of me. Maybe I should push her away, get her out of my life completely. But if she is hiding something from me, keeping her close may be the best way to find out what it is.

My mom comes up to me and hugs me. "Are you sure you don't want to come back to the house? I'd love to get to know your lady friend more."

"Geesh, mom. She's not my lady friend. We're not in our fifties. She's my girlfriend. And for some ridiculous reason she seems to really like me. She's not going anywhere except home today. It's been a tough week." I look over at Russell, who is waiting by the car. "Have the police said anything else to you about Dad?"

Mom deflates and shakes her head. "They can't find him. You know as much as I do. Someone using his passport crossed over the Detroit-Windsor border into the United States and flew out of Detroit airport for Greece."

"Do you have any idea what this Council is? The one that crazy woman Amy mentioned?"

Mom shakes her head. "I always thought I knew your father. After he left . . . well, it was like I never knew the man at all. So many secrets. He should really be here right now."

But I knew there was no way he would be. Amy didn't come right out and say my father was part of some secret organization, but whatever Council Amy's uncle was on, my father must be part of it, too. As far as I'm concerned, the farther away he stays the better.

I walk over to Coyle, Demena and Gabriel. As I approach, they all stop talking.

"Spill it," I say. "I've had enough secrets for one lifetime."

"It's Amy," Coyle says. "She was found in her cell this morning. Dead."

"It appears as if she strangled herself," Demena says. "But . . . I'll deny this if you try leaking it to the press, you understand. My gut tells me she was murdered. People talk in prison."

"That's what I'm hoping for," I say.

Coyle looks at me strangely, and I wave his concern away.

"Never mind." I turn to Gabriel. "Can you give me a ride? Delilah has somewhere else she needs to be."

Gabriel narrows his eyes at me, telling me quite clearly he knows I'm up to something. But he just nods and walks over to his car.

I turn back to Coyle and Demena. "Thank you. You literally saved my life."

"I think you did a good job of saving yourself," Demena says. "Mighty impressive how you broke out of those restraints."

I smile. "That's the power of YouTube. You can learn anything on the internet."

Coyle nods. "We'll keep investigating this Council that Amy's uncle is supposed to be on, but it appears the two of them were acting alone. Lucius Vitalli has been questioned. He has air-tight alibis for the timing of each murder. According to him, he's only seen his niece a few times in the last few years."

Meaning it's basically a dead end. Which is pretty much what I expected.

"Any more word on Paeder Ferris?"

Coyle shakes his head. "Just what I told you yesterday. His picture is all over the media now. We have a twenty-four-hour tip line running but we haven't heard anything conclusive yet."

"We've got reports of him in Vancouver, Calgary and Montreal," Demena says. "Let's hope he headed for a big city. If he goes into the wilds of British Columbia or the Laurentian Mountains, it could take years to find him."

Coyle looked up at the sky. "Looks like it's going to snow again. We should be getting back to the precinct. Keep your eyes open, Clive. Are you sure you want to stay in your old apartment?"

"Not even remotely." I look over at Gabriel. "I'm thinking of making a move. I'm considering asking a friend if he wants to move in together. In a completely different apartment building."

Coyle follows my eyes over to Gabriel. "That's a good idea. If anyone can keep you safe, it's Gabriel Wainright."

And again I feel like an idiot because I still have zero memory of Gabriel's last name. I'm all set to move in with him, and yet I know next to nothing about him. If I'm going to survive in this world, I'm going to have to get smarter. Faster. Stronger. Maybe I don't know everything about Gabriel, but I'm going to have to trust my instinct here. Something tells me I can learn a lot from him.

As I watch Coyle and Demena walk away, I realize something about me has fundamentally changed. Maybe it's because I was taken again, but this time I wasn't a victim. Maybe it's too many hits to the head. I don't know. What I am sure about is this – I'm going to do my damnedest to turn my OCD into a weapon. If I can just find a way to become obsessed with people and practical details instead of useless anxieties, maybe next time I can avoid psychos completely.

Everything seems like it's been wrapped up, but I'm still very unclear on the motivations for some of the deaths. Why was Kevin's body left in an abandoned subway? It seems far too random to actually be, you know, random. It must have had some meaning I can't see. There's no evidence linking Amy and Paeder to the disappearance of Kevin's old boss. And what about Monica? Was she killed just for sport? Because of her connection to Jerry Tran? And what about Melissa? Was it Paeder who took those pictures of her sleeping after her hookup with Kevin? And why did they kill her? Or did someone else do that?

My gut tells me there is another mystery here, one I haven't figured out yet.

Will there be a next time? I put my hand in my pocket and grasp the handle of the asp I stole from Gabriel. Until Paeder and my father are in custody, I'm taking it as a certainty they will come for me again.

And next time I'll be ready.

EPILOGUE

"Are you sure about this?" Gabriel asks.

"For the fifteenth time, yes." I hold my arms out to the side as the prison guard pats me down. Since I didn't want it confiscated, I left Gabriel's asp under the front passenger seat.

We drove up to Kingston last night. Access to this prisoner is limited, but because of Gabriel I didn't have to go through the normal application process. It only took him a few phone calls to get me in.

A guard leads me through the door past an area that looks like a cafeteria. Families are seated at small round tables meeting with inmates. Thankfully, my meeting will be in a much more secure location.

I sit down on the cold plastic chair and look through the thick bulletproof glass in front of me. I touch it, knock on it a few times, just to make sure it's strong enough. This gets me a warning glance from a guard.

"Sorry," I say. "Nerves."

"You got more balls than I do," the guard says. "If I was you, I wouldn't come within a hundred kilometers of this place."

I grin. I'm really not sure this has anything to do with balls. But something is gnawing inside my mind, and I can't stop until, one way or another, I know.

It's nearly another full minute before the guards bring him. I'm not really sure what I was expecting my reaction to be, but I understand almost immediately I'm completely unprepared to see him.

Banner.

He's dressed in an orange jumpsuit, his ankles and wrists shackled together. His hair and beard are shaved, and I can see evidence of scarring around his face and head that weren't there before. Prison, it seems, has not been kind to the child-killer.

He sits down in the chair across from me. And I hear the nail gun. I hear children screaming. I can almost smell his sweat again as he used me like a toy. I start to hyperventilate. The guards on the other side move toward Banner. I stand up, shake my head and motion for them to leave him.

"I've come this far," I say to the guard on my side. "Just give me a few minutes. Please."

The guard nods and motions for his colleagues to back away. It's just me and Banner.

I lift up the phone handset and place it to my ear. A second later, grinning like a hungry man at a buffet, Banner does the same.

"Tell me about the shadows," I say.

Banner laughs. "Why? Have you started to see them?"

"Of course not."

Banner fingers his nipple with his free hand. A guard comes over and knocks his hand away.

I want to ask him if the shadows are real. If the glowing red eyes I saw were the result of being drugged or something else. But I can't bring myself to actually ask the question, not while guards are watching me. If I say the wrong thing to the wrong people, I could end up in a place just like this. So instead I try another question.

"Why did you take me?" I ask.

Banner smiles and motions for me to lean closer. I know there's thick glass between the two of us, but still I hesitate.

The light in the room flickers and he smiles. "I thought you were special." He looks up and over his shoulder at a patch of shadows in the corner of the room. "They told me you might be. But they were wrong. There's nothing special about you."

I lean back in my chair and think about what he's said. Part of me wants to scream that I am special, but the rational part of my mind is winning. So, what if the voices in the psycho's head tell him I'm not special? I just survived an attack by a serial killer.

Far as I'm concerned that makes me something.

Banner pulls the phone away and whispers something to himself. He's looking over in the corner again, but I keep my eyes on him.

"They slip into the world," he says. "They use mirrors like doors between worlds. Soon they will open the door."

"Uh-huh. Well, this has been fun," I say. "So glad I saw you. Seeing how sick and pathetic you are . . . well, I think it will help me move on with my life. Get my head together. Thank you for that. Goodbye, Banner."

He slams an open hand against the glass.

I jump back, and the guards are moving towards us, hands on their weapons.

"Oh, you'll thank me, all right." Banner howls with laughter, his eyes fixated on the shadows in the corner as he speaks to me. "Thank me when the Orpheans rise. Thank me when they slice open your gut and rip out your innards for being such a bad boy. You think you're safe out there? They are everywhere. They see everything. And now their eyes are firmly on you."

He's still looking at the shadows as the guards pulls him away, ranting about the eyes.

I look back at the patch of shadow. And, just for a moment . . .

I see them too.

The End

To find out what happens to Paeder Ferris
and learn more about the Council, read
Council of Peacocks, available now.
Continue reading for a sneak peek.

Clive's adventures will continue in
The Witches of Cuba,
available early 2020.

SNEAK PEEK:

THE STORY CONTINUES IN
COUNCIL OF PEACOCKS

Driving down the dirt road, Josh removed his sunglasses when the sun dropped below the tall pines. They had left Ottawa only two hours ago but this felt like an alien world: pristine and pure. Beside him, his girlfriend, Jan, admired the tree-covered mountains of the Laurentians. The six of them were going to the cabin Jan's parents owned on Lac Manitou. The SUV was filled with enough food and alcohol to tide them over for the three weeks they planned to spend in the woods. Jan's parents had paid for all of it. Money was no object as long as Jan spent it somewhere else.

"Jesus! You drive like an old woman. We should have been there, like, five hours ago."

"What are you? Twelve?" Josh glanced in the rearview mirror at his best friend. Brian was a thick-necked brute with hazel eyes and short brown hair. On a good day, he verged on charming. Today was not one of those days. "Just chill and have another drink?"

"Way ahead of you." Brian smiled and sipped vodka from a Tim Hortons' cup. "It's not the same, though. These cups make the vodka taste like ass."

Josh shook his head. "And yet you still drink it. Says volumes about you. Since I'm an old lady, did you wanna drive for a bit? Oh wait. You can't. Someone lost their license because they were stupid enough to drive drunk."

"Correction." Rebecca, Brian's girlfriend since 10th grade, looked up from her cell phone. Her long, curly brown hair was pulled away from her face to deal with the heat. She sat directly behind Jan. "Someone was stupid enough to get caught drinking and driving. I'm sure he's learned his lesson. Does anyone else have service? My phone just died."

"Maybe it's a sign to put your phone away." Matt

stopped making out with his new girlfriend, Tonia, and leaned forward from the back row of seats. "And for the record, Brian's not really the learning type. Anyone know exactly how many times he's smashed his car into the garage? Anyone? 'Cause, you know, I can't."

"Twice." Brian turned around in his seat and faced Matt. "I did that twice. And it's not like I broke the garage. Bunch of puritans, that's what you are."

Josh reached over and squeezed Jan's hand. She smiled and squeezed back. Then his smile slipped as he remembered the problems back home. For the last six months, his parents' fighting was on a whole new level. Mom accused Dad of having an affair. Dad claimed it was only work that took him away from home. Considering what Dad did, it was feasible.

"You're doing it again." Jan put a hand on his neck and massaged the tension away. She was nearly the physical antithesis of Josh. Every feature on her face hinted at prestige and class. Josh's features were soft and boyish, almost feminine. She kept her black hair in a short bob; his was a thick, blond tangle. The only attribute they shared in common was their light blue eyes. "We agreed no wallowing until we return to civilization, remember?"

Josh turned to her and smiled. "Sorry. Thanks for noticing."

"Not like you're hard to read, Mr. Wilkinson." She released his hand and checked her cell. "You're easily the worst liar I've ever met, which is just fine by me. I have no signal either, Becka. Must be a dead zone."

"Is there coverage at the cabin?" Tonia said as she checked her phone. "My parents will freak if they can't contact me."

"Unfortunately, there is." Jan put her phone away. "We're supposed to be getting away from all this crap. Otherwise, what's the point in camping?"

Moments later, Josh reached down and turned up the music.

"Hey, what's up?" Jan asked. "Don't like my singing?"

"Were you singing?" He pretended to wince as Jan slapped him.

"You know I was. You always do that – turn up the music when I'm singing."

"Really? Must be a coincidence. I just love this song."

Brian kicked the back of Josh's chair. "Since when do you like One Direction, man? Just tell her the truth. No? Fine, then I will. Every time you sing, Josh gets so blinded by his love for you that he just can't drive straight. That's why he's turning up the music."

"Oh please." Matt threw a book at Brian's head. It missed and hit Josh.

"Come on guys! Trying to drive here." Josh yelled into the rear-view mirror. The horseplay wouldn't normally bother him. Maybe Jan was right. Maybe he was letting things back home get to him.

"Oh yeah," Rebecca said as she grabbed Brian's cup. "All this traffic makes it really dangerous. What do you think you'd hit? A moose?"

"Either that or a tree." Josh brushed his sweat-damp hair from his forehead. "I'm not trying to be a buzz kill. Just stop the flying shrapnel, okay?"

Josh turned off onto a road marked with a hand-painted sign. On one side of the road, he caught glimpses of the lake. The trees pushed in further on the road, blocking out even more light.

"Do people actually live up here?" Tonia pushed her glasses back into place and stared out the windows at tall pine trees on either side of the road. "We haven't seen a car or house since we left that creepy gas station."

"What's the matter?" Matt put his arm around Tonia and passed her a wine cooler. "Afraid this is going to turn out to be a little Québécois Chainsaw Massacre thing? Of course people live here. And not the crazy hillbilly type. The guy in the cottage next to ours has a helicopter pad. Tons of celebrities and millionaires buy places out here. You couldn't ask for a safer place. Or maybe," he said leaning forward, fingers curled into claws. "Maybe there are cannibal fur traders just waiting in the woods to…"

The front two tires blew out. With a loud hiss and pop, the SUV swerved off the road.

A sudden rush of adrenaline negated Josh's exhaustion. He fought with the steering wheel to get the SUV back on the asphalt. He knew it was a losing battle even before they hit the tree. Luckily, everyone was wearing their seatbelts. Aside from the burn of the seatbelts against their chests, there were no injuries. The vehicle, however, was totaled. The front end was wrapped firmly around an evergreen.

"Damn." Matt's voice was quiet.

The engine sputtered and died. The wind blew through the trees; birds called out from unseen places. Josh turned off the ignition. He looked over his shoulder at Brian and Matt. Without a word, the men got out of the vehicle to inspect the damage.

"This can't be happening," Matt held his head with both hands. He looked up and down the street. There was still no sign of other cars.

"Your dad is so going to kill you." Brian walked to the front of the SUV and stared at the crunched metal. Slowly and repeatedly, he shook his head.

"How bad is it?" Jan got out of the vehicle, rubbing her chest where the seatbelt had hit.

"Get back in the car," Josh said. He inhaled deeply and knelt to inspect the tires. When he stood, he held two foot-long shards of metal. They were black and tapered, shaped like long feathers. On the wide end was an etching of a peacock.

Matt knelt down and inspected the front tires on the passenger side. "Crap. There's some over here, too."

Jan stared at the daggers still stuck in the passenger-side tire. "It's possible they were just lying in the road."

Josh gave her a very steady look. Then he turned to study the woods.

"Crap." Brian's eyes went wide. "Rebecca, stay in the car." He surveyed the woods on the other side of the road.

Matt looked at Tonia and just shook his head.

"Pull those things out," Josh said. "You're going to need them."

"Stop, Josh. You're freaking me out." Brian's eyes were red.

"Good. We need to be scared. They've done this before. If we don't think straight, we're as good as dead."

"What about you, Josh?" Matt asked. "You're smaller than either of us."

"There's not enough for all of us," Josh said. "I can take care of myself."

"But…?" Matt said.

"Let it go." Brian took one of the daggers, all the while staring at Josh.

"Oh? Had many encounters with crazed woodmen who trap tourists?"

"Not exactly. Let's just say I have a few secrets. We don't have time for this. This is the point in the movies when the disposable teens split up."

"And the body count starts." Matt went pale as soon as he realized what he had just said. He backed up until his shoulders were firmly against the side of the SUV. Tonia knocked on the window and he whirled around. Opening the side door, he passed a shard to each of the women. "We probably won't need these. Just to be safe." Matt smiled. It was thin and unconvincing.

"Safe?" Tonia pressed a hand against her stomach, repulsed as she took the blade.

"We can't stay here," Jan walked over to Josh and grabbed his arm. "We're sitting ducks. They're probably watching us right now. What if they have guns?"

Josh kissed her on the cheek. "If they had guns they probably would've shot the tires out."

"You'd have to be a pretty good shot to hit the tires of a moving car." Jan studied the metal in her hands. "Sharp objects on the road make for better odds."

Rebecca stepped out of the car, blade in hand. "Don't you think we're, like, overreacting or something? Maybe these things just fell off a truck or something."

"Shut up." Josh held up his hand and whispered the word. It was enough to quiet everyone. He walked up the road, eyes down.

"Wait up!" Jan raced after him. "Where are you going? You know we shouldn't split up."

"They shouldn't have gone into the tires like that."

"What do you mean?"

Josh stopped and turned to her. "Sharp pieces of metal lying in the road would tear a hole in the tread. They wouldn't get stuck in like that."

Jan shook her head for a moment. Then she nodded and folded her arms across her chest. "They went in the side of the tires."

Josh nodded. "I doubt they'd be in the sides if we ran over them. Help me look. If someone threw them, there could be others lying around."

Brian walked over from the SUV. "What's going on here, Josh?"

"I don't know."

"Is this like the last time?"

Josh stopped. "What last time? What are you talking about?"

Brian opened his mouth, then sighed and looked at the ground. "Never mind."

"No sign of any others," Jan said.

Josh wiped the sweat from his forehead. "Means they must be really good shots. Didn't miss once."

Brian stiffened and his eyes went wide. "Either that or they ran up to the road and got them back already."

Josh looked at his best friend and his girlfriend.

Jan started to back up. "We should get back."

Josh nodded.

They all walked quickly back to the SUV.

"Are we going?" Rebecca asked.

"We stay," Brian took her in his arms and kissed the top of her head. "It's not much, but the vehicle is the only cover we have. That and the trees. Besides, it's not impossible that another car could drive by. I'm not holding my breath, but it could happen. In theory."

Josh reached into the car to grab his sunglasses. "Why did we take this way again?"

Jan rolled her eyes. "You wanted to try a different route than last year. See new scenery."

"Looks like you got your wish." Rebecca shook her dagger at Josh.

"Yikes." Josh bit his lip and winced. "Sorry. Let's try to get this off the tree." He opened the front passenger door, stepped inside and reached over the wheel. He turned the key a quarter turn until he heard the steering wheel unlock. Then he put the gear in neutral and slid back out. "Tonia, take the wheel. Everyone else, come help. The way it's lodged, we're going to need you."

Within seconds, Tonia was craning her neck to look out the rear window while the other five pushed on the front of the car.

She never saw what hit her.

"Jesus Christ!" Brian screamed as the driver's side window exploded. Glass fragments blasted everywhere. Instinctively, everyone covered their faces and closed their eyes.

Josh dropped to the ground. He pulled the others by their shorts and beltlines until all were lying flat in the underbrush. Matt wheezed, an asthmatic sound. His body went through a steady string of spasms. As he stared into nothing, his lips worked their way around Tonia's name.

"Stay." Josh gripped Jan's shoulder, making it an order rather than a plea. He crawled on his stomach toward the road; each breath was hot and painful. "Please don't be dead," he whispered to himself. He hoped it'd been a rock, a bird, anything but another of those shards. A shard would mean blood and death. He got off his stomach when he reached the road, using the SUV for protection. He opened the passenger door as quietly as he could and peeked inside at Tonia's body.

"Blood and death." Her neck was twisted at an unnatural angle. The impact had snapped her spine. A six-inch black blade – identical to the ones in the tires – had slammed into the lower left section of her skull. A part of him, a dark part that spoke to him more often than he wanted to admit, told him to take the shard out of her head. It was a weapon and he was going to need it. One thought of Matt and he knew he couldn't do it.

He climbed into the SUV and pushed Tonia's body back up in the driver's seat. He crouched down near the floor and used her body as cover. He wasn't a big man. Her body wouldn't have been much protection for Matt or Brian.

Josh moved to roll down the driver's side window. When his fingers touched glass fragments on the window control, he realized what he was doing. There was no window anymore.

"Brian," he said as calmly as he could.

After a moment he heard a very quiet answer. "Is she...?"

"Not now. Keep Matt down. Don't let him see this. I want you all to stay on your knees but try to push the van backwards. I'll steer."

"Are you crazy?" Jan said. "You'll be killed."

"Not. Now. I'm okay. Don't think about what I'm doing. Just focus on pushing this thing backwards. Do it now."

He didn't expect it to work. The four of them, even Matt, were on their knees pushing the vehicle off the tree. The SUV shuddered, then, unexpectedly, pushed forcefully off the tree.

"Stay down," he said out the window. "Use the trees for protection. We know where they are now." He lied for their peace of mind more than anything. Panic would get someone else killed. He turned the key in the ignition. The engine sputtered and complained. "I need a miracle now. Right now. Come on."

The engine sparked into life. He was in the middle of breathing a sigh of relief when he saw movement out of the corner of his eye. He looked into the woods. Three dark shadows raced toward them.

Josh yelled out the window. "Get in! Now!" Maybe it was something in his voice or some sound they heard from the woods, but they all followed his lead. Still crouched over, they raced through the side doors. Josh didn't wait for the doors to close before he drove off.

To continue reading,
get your copy of
Council of Peacocks today.

Praise for *M Joseph Murphy*

"Murphy writes in a vein similar to
the older works of Stephen King.
His writing is intense, creative,
and imaginative."

- MICHELLE S. WILLMS,

"Fans of dark fantasy, urban fantasy
and horror should love this
fast-paced novel chocked full of
mayhem, chaos, destruction, and
snappy one-liners."

- TRAVIS LUEDKE,
New York Times Best Selling
Author of *The Nightlife Series*

"A brilliant dark fantasy thriller
that reads like a Robert Rodriguez
movie - Desperado meets
From Dusk Till Dawn."

- SIMON OKILL
Author of the gothic classic
Luna Sanguis

WORKS BY M JOSEPH MURPHY

ACTIVATION SERIES
Council of Peacocks
Beyond the Black Sea
Terra Incognita

SWORD OF KASSANDRA SERIES
A Fallen Hero Rises
Demons of Dundegore
The Backward Pawn (Coming summer 2020)

CLIVE DUFAULT MYSTERIES
Are you Watching Me?
The Witches of Cuba (Coming spring 2020)

ABOUT M JOSEPH MURPHY

Joseph Murphy was born and raised in Ontario, Canada. He earned his geekdom at an early age. He read X-Men comics from at the age of eight, and it only went downhill from there.

As a teenager he wrote short stories and wanted to be the next Stephen King. Instead of horror, however, he kept writing fantasy stories. After surviving high school as a goth with a purple mohawk, he studied English and Creative Writing at the University of Windsor.

He lives in Windsor, Ontario, Canada (right across the stream from Detroit, Michigan) with his husband and a shy-but-friendly ghost.

www.ingramcontent.com/pod-product-compliance
Lightning Source LLC
Chambersburg PA
CBHW070919260626
47162CB00007B/2734